Gym Class Can Be Murder

"Hiya, Coach," I said. "How's a guy go about joining the football team?"

He put down his sandwich. "What guy are we talking about?" he rumbled.

"Uh, me."

Coach belched gently. It sounded like someone in the cafeteria had dropped a hand grenade in the haggis. "Don't make me laugh," he said.

I thought of mentioning that I'd actually made him burp, but decided against it.

"No, really," I said. "I'd like to play."

"You'd get creamed out there," he said.

"Let me worry about that." (Believe me, I was plenty worried.)

"Hmm." Coach pondered, and his eyebrows flexed like little weight lifters. "But you're not even in sixth grade," he said.

"I'm old for my age."

Coach Stroganoff put both meaty paws on the desk. "Meet me at the gym right after school."

I grinned, nodded my thanks, and turned to go.

"Oh, and Gecko," he said. "Remember to tell my assistant your next of kin."

This Gum for Hire

Chet Gecko Mysteries

The Chameleon Wore Chartreuse
The Mystery of Mr. Nice
Farewell, My Lunchbag
The Big Nap
The Hamster of the Baskervilles
This Gum for Hire
The Malted Falcon

And coming soon

Trouble Is My Beeswax
Give My Regrets to Broadway
Murder, My Tweet

This Gum for Hire

FROM THE TATTERED CASEBOOK OF

CHET GECKO
PRIVATE EYE

Bruce Hale

HARCOURT, INC.

Orlando • Austin • New York • San Diego • Toronto • London

Requests for permission to make copies of any part of the
work should be mailed to the following address:
Permissions Department, Harcourt, Inc.,
6277 Sea Harbor Drive, Orlando, Florida 32887-6777.

www.HarcourtBooks.com

First Harcourt paperback edition 2003
First published 2002

The Library of Congress has cataloged
the hardcover edition as follows:
Hale, Bruce.
This gum for hire: from the tattered casebook of Chet
Gecko, private eye/by Bruce Hale.
p.   cm.
"A Chet Gecko Mystery."
Summary: To save his own skin, private eye Chet Gecko
sets out to solve the mystery of Emerson Hicky
Elementary School's disappearing football players.
[1. Football—Fiction.   2. Schools—Fiction.
3. Geckos—Fiction.   4. Animals—Fiction.
5. Humorous stories.   6. Mystery and detective stories.]
I. Title.
PZ7.H1295Th   2002
[Fic]—dc21   2001008127
ISBN 0-15-202491-3
ISBN 0-15-202497-2 pb

Text set in Bembo
Display type set in Elroy
Designed by Ivan Holmes

C E G H F D

Printed in the United States of America

For Michael, eagle-eyed editor and partner in crime. Couldn't have done it without ya

This Gum for Hire

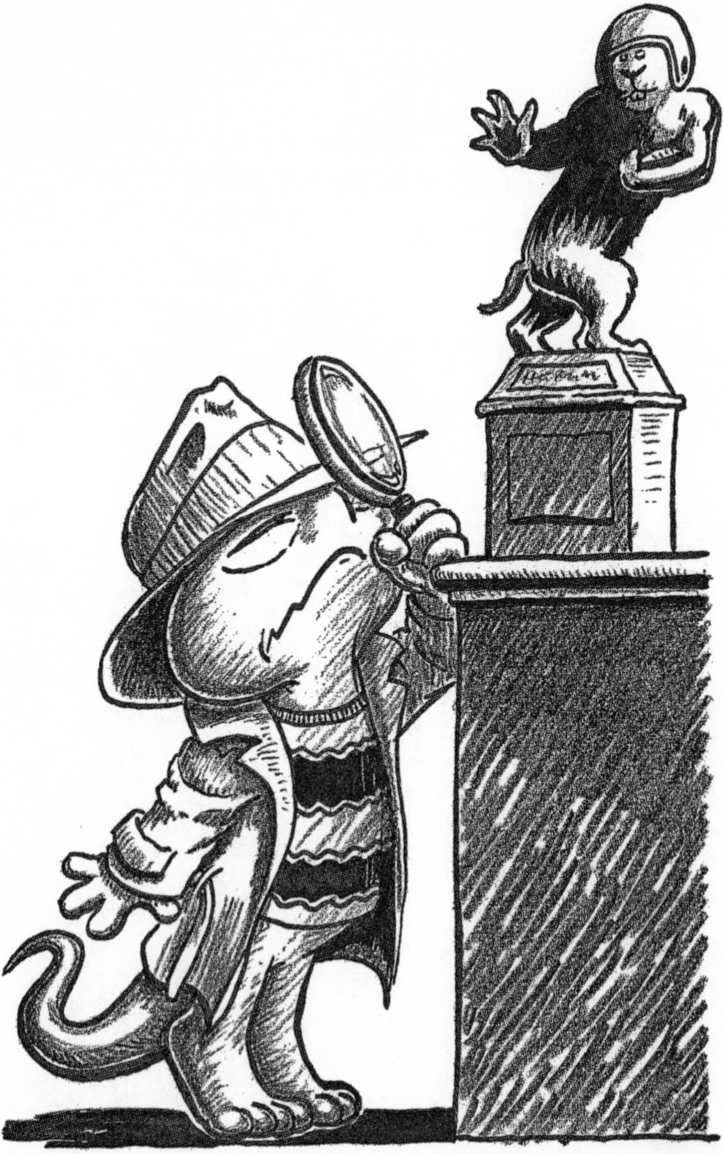

A private message from the private eye ...

My workout philosophy has always been a simple one: no pain, no pain. You won't find me trying out for soccer, baseball, or basketball, because I'm not big on team sports (or even individual sports, for that matter).

Fact is, I'd rather work out the angles of a mystery than work out at the gym any day. Of course, you'd expect that from a private eye. That's me: Chet Gecko, best lizard detective at Emerson Hicky Elementary.

Don't get me wrong—I like exercise. I could sit and watch other people do it all day. But this one case gave me more action than I could handle. It plunged me deeper into the sports world than a dung beetle in elephant poop.

I thought the case was a slam dunk. But as I struck out on one clue after another, the trail led me straight to my least favorite place on earth: P.E. class.

And there I learned the truth about sports: If you watch a game, it's fun; if you play it, it's recreation; if you work at it, it's football.

1

Case of the Mopey Monster

The stink alone should have tipped me off. I was taking a brain break, just swinging on the swing set, when a serious stench grabbed me in its funky blue fist.

It was strong enough to make a skunk blush.

Hmm, I thought, as I *whoosh*ed forward. *Cabbage and beans for breakfast?*

Right stink, wrong source.

Something snagged me in midswing—*glomp!*—and there I hung, stuck in the sky.

I twisted to look under the seat. An ugly mug met my gaze.

Even wrong way around, I could tell: It was Herman the Gila Monster. He wasn't as big as Beijing,

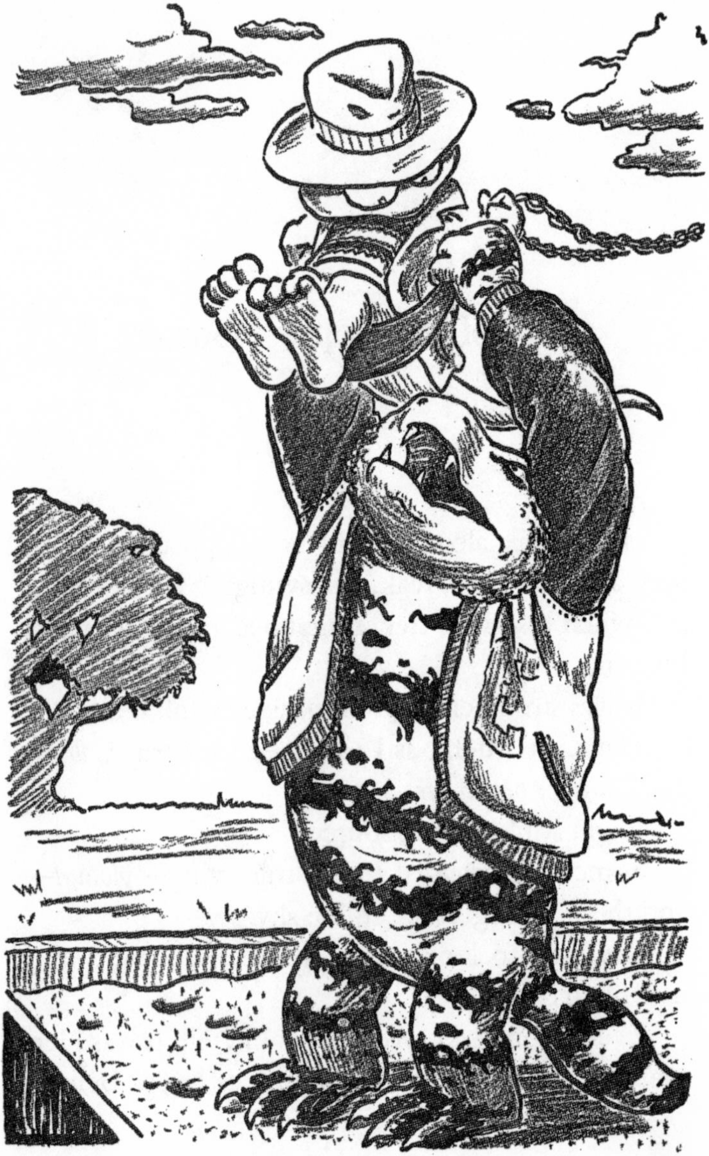

he wasn't as mean as a six-pack of hungry sharks. But the Big Bad Wolf could've learned something from Herman—his breath was stinky enough to melt a brick house.

"What's up, Herman?" I asked, coughing.

"You," he said.

That's Gila monster humor for you.

Normally, I kept my distance from the big lug. But since he'd already caught me, my best move was to play dumb.

Unfortunately, you can't play dumber than Herman without a lobotomy.

"You wanted to see me?" I asked.

"Yup," he said, hoisting me by my tail. "I like talk."

I almost told him, *Go see a speech doctor,* but it was a long way down to the ground.

"I talk better on my feet," I said.

"Okay." Herman let go my tail.

The ground rushed up to meet me like a car salesman at closing time.

Whonk!

As I climbed to my feet, the burly Gila monster clapped a hand onto my shoulder. "We go . . . someplace private," Herman growled.

My life flashed before me. It wasn't pretty. But it was *my* life, darn it, and I wanted to live to see fifth grade.

"Let's go to the scrofulous tree," I said. "I do my best thinking there."

With a grunt, the Gila monster steered me in that direction. Two small squirrels were playing Frisbee under my favorite tree.

"Scram!" Herman growled.

They scrammed. Herman shoved me down on the grass. I rolled and raised my fists and feet, ready to fight back. Then, with a thud like a meteorite hitting the earth, the Gila monster flopped down beside me.

"Gecko," he said, "I got problem."

"I've been meaning to mention that," I said. "You know, a little mouthwash—"

"Not funny," he rumbled. "Problem big."

I sat up. He was serious.

I'd never figured myself as a friendly ear for school-yard thugs, but what the heck. I bit.

"What's on your mind?" I asked. "And I use that term loosely."

Herman sighed like an avalanche on a distant mountain. "Team in trouble. Coach blame me."

The Gila monster was a fearsome football player. Several times, he'd been kicked off the team for his hijinks, but he always got called back. Emerson Hicky Elementary took its sports seriously, and a monster on the front line is hard to find.

Like I cared about that.

"So," I asked, "why tell me?"

Herman's heavy head swung my way. "Players go bye-bye," he said. "Not my fault. Gecko can find players."

"Oh, no," I said. "Not me."

Herman moved faster than a starving toad at a fruit-fly fest. Before I could even twitch, he grabbed my ankle.

"Gecko will help," he growled. "Or Gecko will *need* help." The Gila monster shook his other fist meaningfully. I got the picture.

Then, a thought took that long, lonely trip across Herman's mind. His fangs twinkled in a smile. "Plus, Herman will pay. One chocolate cake for every player you find."

I smiled back. "That should've been the first thing you said, buddy boy. Tell the nice detective all about it."

2

Cakey Breaky Heart

I paced under the scrofulous tree while Herman spilled his guts. (Not literally; even a Gila monster isn't *that* disgusting.)

The football team had begun disappearing, lunk by lunk. Players didn't show up for practice, didn't turn up in class. Coach "Beef" Stroganoff, being the understanding type, blamed Herman.

"Not my fault," Herman repeated. "I never scare them off."

This big hunk of bad news *had* terrorized plenty of kids over the years. But a glimmer of sincerity in his beady black eyes made me believe him.

"How long have the players been disappearing?" I asked.

"Since last week," he grunted. "Hugh gone on Wednesday."

"Anyone else vanish?"

His mouth hung open in thought. "Uh, Lou on Thursday. Dewey Friday."

I frowned. "You mean you've lost Hughey, Louie, and Dewey?"

"Yeah."

"Then it must be hard to get your ducks in a row."

"What?" he asked.

"Never mind. Are you sure these guys disappeared?"

Herman scratched his head. It sounded like a file grating on granite. "They never come to practice."

I spread my hands. "So . . . did the coach call their parents?"

The Gila monster glowered. "Duh," he said. "Coach no dummy. Players not at home, not at school. All gone."

I smiled a little, in spite of myself. This *was* a mystery.

"Not funny," said Herman. "Coach kick Herman off team if players not back Thursday."

"What's the big deal?" I asked. "You've been tossed off the football team more often than I've snagged the last brownie on the plate."

Herman looked down. "Big game Friday."

True, we were playing the low-down sultans of stinkeroo, Petsadena Elementary. But he wasn't telling me the whole story.

"And so . . . ," I said, trying to draw him out.

The Gila monster glanced left and right. "Must play," he muttered. "Girlfriend coming to game."

Girlfriend?! Eeew. The thought turned my stomach. What kind of girl would go for a thug like Herman?

But then, what kind of sap would want a girl to go for him in the first place? Mysteries, mysteries everywhere.

Herman clenched his fist and glared. "Find players or . . ." He didn't need to spell it out (which was good, 'cause he couldn't spell).

"I'm on it," I said. Just then, my stomach growled. "Hey, any chance for a couple of pieces of cake as a retainer?"

Herman growled back.

"I'll take that as a no." I turned and started off across the playground. Touchy-touchy, these clients.

3

Another Brick in the Chuckwalla

It's hard to just sit in Mr. Ratnose's class when there's a case afoot. Of course, it's hard to just sit in Mr. Ratnose's class, period.

Still, the minutes passed, as minutes will. Lunchtime found me on a bench by the krangleberry trees, munching a peanut butter 'n' dragonfly sandwich and nibbling a Lice Krispie treat.

I was working on a wing and waiting on a dame. I didn't have long to wait.

"What do ya know, Eskimo?" squawked a cheerful voice.

"Not much, er . . . double-Dutch," I said.

It was my partner, Natalie Attired, a spiffy mockingbird with a detective sense sharp enough to cut cheese. (Not that I like friends cutting the cheese around me.) She *plonk*ed down and dug into her own lunch—a sesame seed–and–earthworm casserole.

Bird food, again.

"Hey," said Natalie, "I just heard the best new joke. What's made of plastic and hangs around French cathedrals?"

I braced myself. "I dunno, what?"

"The lunchpack of Notre Dame." She giggled.

I groaned. "Listen," I said, "you want to work on your comedy act, or you want to do some sleuthing? We've got a case."

A sparkle lit my partner's eyes. "Really? Who's the client?"

"Herman the Gila Monster."

Natalie reared back and spread her wings. "Chet, I think *you've* got a case—of amnesia. Didn't Herman try to marinate us in chlorine a while back?"

"Yeah, but—"

"And tie your tail in a knot just last week?"

I held up my hands. "Yeah, but he's paying us in cake."

My partner sat back, her feathers settling. "Why didn't you say so? What's the case?"

I ran down what I knew so far.

Natalie pecked at her casserole. "Let's see . . . why did these players disappear?" she mused.

"They all ran off together to play hooky?"

"Maybe," she said. "Or...someone was trying to get Herman in trouble?"

"Maybe," I said. "But there's one thing wrong with that theory."

"What?"

"Too many suspects. Everyone hates Herman."

"Good point," she said. We ate awhile.

An idea struck me in midcrunch. I pointed a Lice Krispie at Natalie. "Or...what if someone had a grudge against football players and kidnapped them?"

Natalie stopped eating. "*Hmm*. I like that theory. So who's got something against football players?"

We stared at each other, but nothing came.

"I don't know," I said. "But I know who would know."

"Who do you know who would know?"

"You know: Coach Stroganoff."

Coach "Beef" Stroganoff put the *meat* in meathead. A massive, crew-cut groundhog, he was as charming and graceful as a monster-truck rally on a muddy day. Although Coach Stroganoff had a tendency to hibernate when football season wasn't going well, he ruled the gym like a furry emperor.

We found him on the field advising a ragged group of soccer players.

"No, Tiffany!" he yelled. "Kick the ball, not his—"

"Coach Stroganoff!" I called. "Can we talk?"

He turned a heavy, bewhiskered face on us. "Huh? G'wan, I'm busy."

"But—"

A sleek, well-muscled chuckwalla eased off the bench and pulled us aside. "Never bother Coach when he's working," he said. "Catch him after he eats."

"Thanks for the tip," I said, "Mister . . . ?"

"Schortz. Jim Schortz," said the handsome lizard. "But you can call me Jim, dude."

"Thanks, Jim dude," said Natalie. She smiled up at him until her dimples grew dimples. "And what are you, his head quarterback?"

Our new buddy Jim puffed out his chest, stretching his gold lamé shirt. "Nah, I'm the assistant coach—ol' Beef's right-hand lizard."

Jim palmed a rubber ball and began to squeeze, making his arm muscles dance like spastic chickens at a hoedown. Jocks.

I tried to ignore his flexing. "So," I said. "You and the coach must be pretty pumpset—er, upset over the missing football players."

The chuckwalla's eyebrows drew together like lonely kindergartners in the fog. "Whoa, how did you know about that?" he asked.

"News travels fast," I said. "Is it true?"

He chewed a leathery lip. "Yep. We're at our wits' end."

You didn't have far to go crossed my mind. But my mouth said, *"Hmm."*

Natalie batted her eyes. "Maybe we can help."

"And who might you be?" asked Jim.

I squared my shoulders and curled my tail. "We might be Kareem Abdul-Jabbar and Hardy Har-Har," I said. "But sadly, we're not. I'm Chet Gecko, and this is—"

"Natalie Attired," said my partner. "*So* pleased to meet you." She cast the chuckwalla another dewy-eyed look.

Any more of that and I'd be ready to upchuck-walla. Natalie was getting almost as flirty as Frenchy LaTrine.

"What she's trying to say is we're detec—uh, we know about situations like this." No need for Mr. Schortz to hear we were working for his team's number-one bad boy, Herman the Gila Monster.

Jim sat on the bench. Natalie and I leaned in.

"The guys who disappeared," I said, "did they have any enemies?"

"Dunno," said the assistant coach. "Maybe on the other schools' teams?"

Natalie bent close enough to smooch him. "Did they have anything in common?"

"Um, they all played football."

This guy was as sharp as a pencil—the eraser end, anyway.

"Anything else?" I asked.

Natalie's beak parted. Unless something stopped her, she was about to lay a juicy one on Jim. *Yuck.*

"Heads up!" someone cried.

Natalie began to straighten, then—*bonk, whap!*—a speeding soccer ball conked her on the noggin and ricocheted into Jim's face, sending them both sprawling.

I shook my head. Mushy stuff will knock you for a loop every time.

4

Neither a Burrower nor a Lender Be

Science class passed as pleasantly as it always did—like spending an hour napping on a bed of nails.

Recess came, and not a minute too soon. As my classmates stampeded for the door, I shouldered between them, bound for the office. I needed to get the lowdown on the missing players.

As luck would have it, a student in a football jacket was just leaving Principal Zero's lair, rubbing his furry behind. The spanking machine must've been repaired.

I called out to the broad-shouldered squirrel. "Hey there, ace. Got a minute?"

He turned half-lidded eyes on me. "What?" he grunted.

"I wonder if we could talk about your missing teammates?"

"I wunner if you can fly widout wings," the squirrel sneered, flexing his clawed fingers.

"Easy, big fella," I said. "I just want some info."

"What makes it your beeswax?" he said.

"I'm a detective; Herman hired me."

"Yeah, right." He lumbered past.

"Wait!" I said. "Were you close to the players who disappeared?"

The squirrel turned. "Yup," he said. Then he spun and limped off.

Dang. I would have to work on my interviewing technique.

I reached the office door. Maybe I'd have better luck with the principal's secretary, Maggie Crow. She had a soft spot for private eyes.

I poked my head into her office.

"Whaddaya want?" she squawked. "I'm a busy bird."

So much for the soft spot.

"I'm on a case," I said.

"Well, whoop-de-do. What's it to me?"

"I need some information. Can you pull the files on three football players?"

Ms. Crow crossed her wings. "That's classified, buddy boy. School property."

"I'll make it worth your while. Say...a worm sandwich?"

"What?" she said.

"A fistful of worms?"

"Don't make me laugh."

"A bucketful of worms and a year's subscription to *Better Crows & Garbage*?"

She leaned forward. "What did you want to know?"

I left the office with three computer printouts—partial school records for the missing players. (Not even a truckload of worms could coax Maggie Crow into revealing *all* her secrets.)

Ambling along, I began scanning the sheets—until I hit a brick wall.

Fwomp! Papers and hat went flying.

It was Herman. Planted in front of me like a building with a bad attitude—my client, the lovable Gila monster.

I caught my balance and straightened my hat.

"Gecko," he growled. "You find players?"

"Um, not yet, big guy. But the wheels are in motion."

This wasn't a fib; I actually had been spinning my wheels so far.

Herman the Gila Monster wasn't big on trust. He was just big. A hand the size of a cafeteria tray reached down and hoisted me by my shirtfront.

"Tick tock, Gecko," said its owner. "Find players fast. If Coach kick me off team, I kick you off planet."

He wasn't subtle, but he was effective.

"I'll keep you informed."

Herman grunted and set me down without breaking me. I picked up my papers and hurried off to share the players' files with Natalie, just down the hall.

"You take Lou's and Dewey's teachers; I'll take Hugh's," I said, passing over their records.

"Roger, dodger," said Natalie.

"Oh, and by the way," I said. "You owe Maggie Crow a bucketful of worms."

"What?" Natalie's feathers ruffled. "Why?"

"Information doesn't come cheap."

Hugh's record revealed his teacher's name: Ms. Burrower. She was a big mole, with fur soft as a pre-schooler's snore and a nose like a celery stalk caught in a blender.

Ms. Burrower was punishing homework papers with a red pencil when I slipped into her classroom.

"Why, it's wee Chet Gecko," she said. "What brings you here, lad?"

"My two wee feet," I said. "But enough small talk; I need the hot scoop."

She pushed her Coke-bottle glasses up her nose with a thick foreclaw. "What's the subject?"

"Your student, Hugh Geste. He took a powder last week, and no one's seen him since."

The mole's brow wrinkled. "Took a powder?" she asked.

"Vanished, split, went on the lam," I said.

"Ah, yes. He's not in school." She didn't seem particularly worried about it.

I stepped close to her desk. "Tell me, did he have any enemies?"

"I shouldn't think so. Hugh was smart and well liked."

I gnawed my lip. "*Hmm.* Was he acting strangely before he disappeared?"

Ms. Burrower chewed her pencil and squinted. "Not that I recall. But I wouldn't call it disappearing. He just went—"

Brrring! Recess ended not with a bang, but with a ding-a-ling.

"What were you going to say?" I asked.

"Nothing important," said the mole. "Back to class with you, lad."

I left, wondering what could make a burly beaver vanish before the biggest game of his football career.

I didn't think I'd like the answer. But I knew I'd find it before long, or my name isn't wee Chet Gecko.

5

Stroganoff the Wall

The last classes of the day sped by like a chariot pulled by crippled snails. Maybe it was my imagination, but Mr. Ratnose even seemed to be speaking extra slowly.

Finally, he droned, "Claaaasss dismiiissssed."

Foom! Life shot into fast motion like a spider launched from a slingshot. I popped out the door behind my classmates. The halls rang with the jibber-jabber of happy students heading for home.

I had heavier duties. A detective's work is never done.

Natalie caught up to me. "I talked to Lou's and Dewey's teachers," she said.

"And?"

We strolled toward the football field and chewed over what we'd learned so far. It made for a small snack.

Like me, Natalie had drawn a blank. The teachers reported no lurking enemies, no suspicious behavior.

"Just one odd thing," she said. "Lou's teacher said she hoped he was enjoying camp."

"*Camp?* Since when is kidnapping camp?" I shook my head. "They've got to stop serving that funky Jell-O in the teachers' lounge."

Natalie and I rounded the gym. Just over the fence, the cheerleaders sweated through their routines. Beyond them, a bunch of kids ran laps, and Coach Stroganoff supervised two players doing wobbly push-ups.

It didn't look like much fun. But then, exercise never does.

We passed through a gate in the wire fence and stepped out onto the track. Bulky football players jogged past. Sweat covered them like chocolate sauce on a banana-slug split.

"Yuck," I said. "I wouldn't do that for love or lunch."

Natalie arched an eyebrow. "You know, you could stand to get a little exercise, Mr. Sowbug Twinkie–muncher."

I ignored her, watching the joggers. "Man, those guys must *hate* Coach Stroganoff."

Natalie's eyes went wide. She clapped her head. "That's it!" she said. "I just had an idea."

"See, there's a first time for everything."

"Chet, what if the kidnapper didn't have a grudge against the players?"

"Huh?"

Natalie pointed at the coach. "What if he had something against *Coach Stroganoff* instead?"

I turned to her. "That's why we couldn't find their enemies. Good thinking, partner."

Just then, the coach in question grimaced at us, then *clomp*ed over like a mountain with legs.

"You there!" he bellowed. "State your name and business."

"Chet Gecko," I said. "Trouble is my business."

Natalie raised a wing feather in greeting. "Natalie Attired. His business is my business."

"Hang on," said Coach Stroganoff. "His business is your business, and your business is his business?" He scratched his jaw. "I can see how that would be trouble."

"We're just nosing around," said Natalie helpfully.

The coach's eyes went wide. "Nosing?" he growled. "Who said you could do that?" He towered over us, a groundhog big enough to hog a small country.

"Um, the nostril fairy?" I said.

"Who knows?" Natalie said.

Coach Stroganoff put two paws the size of milk jugs on his furry hips. "Yeah?" he said. "Well, this is my field; keep away from my team."

"But we're trying to help find—" said Natalie.

"I don't care if you're studying sit-ups for the Abdominal Snowman," said the coach. "Only football players and cheerleaders on the field during practice."

He grabbed us both by the scruff of our necks and marched us to the fence. Easy as stinkbug pie, he lofted us over.

I watched Coach stomp off. "Well, that's that," I grumped. "Now, how do we find out what happened to Hugh, Lou, and Dewey?"

Natalie smiled a thoughtful smile. "I've got an idea," she said, "but you're not going to like it."

"Nonsense. Lay it on me."

6

Team & Sympathy

"No way!" I said. "Never in a million years!"

Natalie grabbed my shoulders and spun me back to face her. "Come on, Chet. It's perfect. How else can you get next to the coach and players?"

"Have you lost your marbles?" I said. "I can't join the football team! It's, it's . . . un–detective-y."

"That's why it'll work," said Natalie. "They won't suspect a thing."

"But I hate the game!"

She smiled sweetly. "I heard that the players get free bubble gum."

Free gum?

"*Hmm*, that's—wait a minute. I can't even *play* football."

"Neither can most of the team. Why do you think they have a 2–15 win-loss record?"

She had a point (other than the one at the end of her beak). The Emerson Hicky Gophers weren't exactly the winningest bunch on the planet. Heck, they made the Bad News Bears look like Super Bowl champs (and the Bears were a baseball team). Still, that was no reason for me to get trompled trying to solve a case.

My tail twitched as I paced. "*Unh-uh,* sister. I'm not joining that team. I'd rather play patty-cake with the cheerleaders in..."

A thought struck me. "Oh, Natalie?"

"Hmm?"

"Just what will *you* be up to while I'm getting the bugs squished out of me on the football field?"

She shrugged. "Guess I'll do some research, snoop for clues."

I smiled. "I don't think so."

Of course, it was one thing to say we'd join the football team and cheerleading squad. It was another matter to pull it off.

Both outfits had at least *some* standards. I didn't think we stood the chance of a balloon at a porcupine picnic. But we had to try.

Carrying a brown paper sack, I visited Coach Stroganoff's office at lunchtime the next day. He was sitting behind his desk, gnawing on a sandwich the size of a sofa.

"Hiya, Coach," I said. "How's a guy go about joining the football team?"

He put down the sandwich. "What guy are we talking about?" he rumbled.

"Uh, me."

Coach belched gently. It sounded like someone in the cafeteria had dropped a hand grenade in the haggis. "Don't make me laugh," he said.

I thought of mentioning that I'd actually made him burp, but decided against it.

"No, really," I said. "I'd like to play."

He did laugh then. Longer and louder than absolutely necessary.

It wasn't *that* funny.

I crossed my arms. "I'll have you know I'm the fastest gecko in my class."

Coach laughed even harder, pounding his desk and smooshing his sandwich.

I took a deep breath. "Look," I said. "You're three players short, and the big game is Friday. You could use some help."

Coach Stroganoff stopped laughing. His forehead wrinkled. For a long moment, the mammoth groundhog stared at me.

"Give me one good reason why I should let you join the team," he said.

I opened the sack and held it out. "Here's ten."

His eyes widened at the sight of ten fresh-baked vanilla Grubworm Dream bars. I'd have to wash dishes for a month, but it was worth it. My mom's treats are irresistible.

"Hmm." Coach snatched the bag. He pondered, and his eyebrows flexed like little weight lifters. "But you're not even in sixth grade," he said.

"I'm old for my age."

Coach Stroganoff put both meaty paws on the desk. "Meet me at the gym right after school."

I grinned, nodded my thanks, and turned to go.

"Oh, and Gecko," he said. "Remember to tell my assistant your next of kin."

7

No Nurse Is Good Nurse

The afternoon flitted by like a butterfly stapled to a desktop.

I was resting my heavy head on my hands, listening to Mr. Ratnose make math even more confusing, when it hit me. That needle-sharp voice.

"Chet Gecko," he said. "If you had twenty cents, and you asked your grandfather for thirty and your grandmother for thirty more, how much would you have?"

"Twenty cents."

The tall rat's whiskers twitched. "Young Gecko, you don't know your math."

"Mr. Ratnose, you don't know my grandparents."

He stared at me, clenched his teeth, and moved on to the next victim.

I checked the clock. One and a half hours till football practice. *Drat.* I had leads to follow up on, and class was cramping my style.

Hmm . . . cramps?

I doubled over, grabbing my gut. *"Oooh,"* I groaned.

Shirley Chameleon leaned across the aisle. "Chet?" she whispered. "Are you all right?"

I sneaked a peek at Mr. Ratnose. He hadn't noticed me.

"OOOOH!" I groaned louder.

Heads turned my way. Mr. Ratnose got the message.

"Chet Gecko?" he said. "Is something the matter?"

I mustered all my acting skills. "I don't feel so good, teacher. My stomach."

Mr. Ratnose narrowed his eyes. *"Hmph!* Probably too many cockroach cupcakes, if I know you."

Nevertheless, he scrawled on his blue pad, tore off the top sheet, and handed it to me. "Go straight to the nurse's office," he said. "And I want to see a note from her explaining your condition."

"Oooh-kay," I moaned. Bent double like a question mark, I shuffled out the door. Just for kicks, I shot Shirley a wink as I passed.

The school nurse, Marge Supial, saw busted-up football players on a regular basis. Maybe she'd talked to the missing players; maybe she had a clue for me.

(One thing was for sure: She had termite lollipops for each visitor—something every growing gecko needs.)

In the nurse's office, a kindergartner slumped on the lumpy brown examination table, homesick and weepy eyed. I scanned the room. No nurse.

Marge Supial's file cabinet beckoned. She probably wouldn't mind if I took a quick peek at the players' files....

The drawer slid open with a soft *shhick*. I paged through the folders, looking for Hugh, Lou, or Dewey. A rumpled pink envelope caught my eye. Being a snoop by nature, I checked out the letter inside.

Dearest Smootchie-Poo,
    I count the minutes until I can groom the fleas from your soft fur, and—

Ugh. A love note. And it was signed *Your Beefie-Pie.*

Hmmm. I knew someone named Beef. Could it be...? *Nah.*

Hugh's file turned up. I had just flipped it open when—

"Here we are, love, a lollipop for—eh? Who's this?"

There was nowhere to run, nowhere to hide. I was busted.

8

Wombattle-ax

I grabbed my gut, spun, and nudged the file cabinet shut with my tail. My eyes met a wombat's furry belly button. "*Oooh,* Nurse, I have a stomach-ache."

"Do you now?" said Marge Supial. "And what were you looking for in there?" She pointed at the file cabinet.

"Um, a cure?"

The nurse plopped a sucker in the kindergartner's mouth, patted her head, and showed her the door. She steered me toward the table. "Sit," she said.

I sat. While Ms. Supial fetched her instruments, I gave her the once-over. She was a gray-haired wombat with regal bearing and steely gray eyes. Imagine the Queen of England with a stethoscope, fuzzy ears, and a nose like an eggplant—you get the picture.

She turned, wielding a tongue depressor like a scepter. "Open!"

I opened my trap. She planted the stick on my tongue while she probed my mouth with a miniature flashlight thingy.

"Hmph!" she sniffed. "Have you had plenty of leafy greens lately?"

"Tho," I said.

"Been eating lots of fried foods?"

"Theth," I said.

Marge Supial fixed me with a stare harder than week-old cafeteria biscuits. "And why is that?" she asked.

"They thayss thoogh."

She removed the tongue depressor and began prodding my gut. "That's no reason to eat such swill."

Her poking began to tickle.

"Fried foods—*hee hee*—can't be bad," I said. "They're fried in vegetable—*ha ha*—oil, aren't they?"

"I suppose," she said.

"And vegetables—*hee*—are good..."

She frowned and gave my stomach another prod. "Yes."

"So why—*ho ho*—aren't fried foods good?"

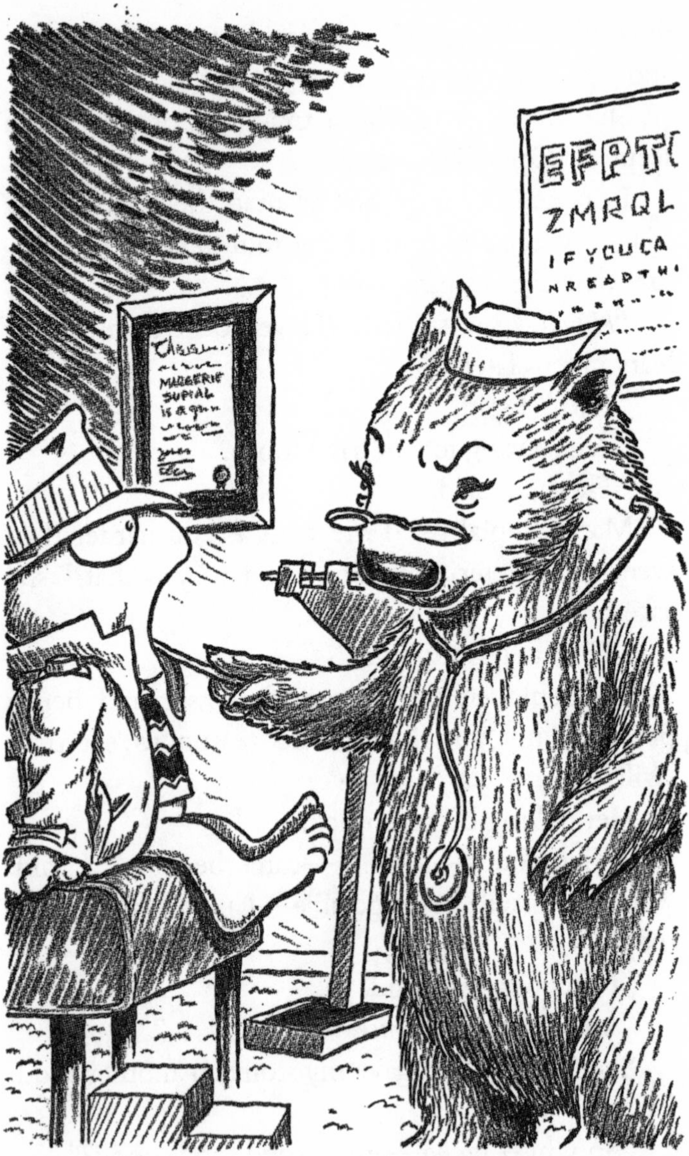
EFPT
ZMRQL
IFYOUCA
NREADTH

Marge Supial stopped poking and frowned. "Why are you here, really?"

I gave her my best Bambi-goes-to-preschool look. "What do you mean?"

"You've got a cast-iron stomach," she said. "You wouldn't get sick if you ate a wallpaper-and-Brillo-pad sandwich. What gives?"

I shrugged. "Got me, sister. I'm here on a case."

She didn't toss me out on my ear, so I continued. "Some football players have done a vanishing act. You might know something."

Marge Supial's face was harder to read than schoolbooks in the summer. She looked like the critter that modeled for the Sphinx.

The wombat folded her arms. "All right, three questions only."

Three questions? I'd have to make them count.

"Um, okay," I said. "Three guys—Hugh, Lou, and Dewey—have disappeared. Did they come in recently?"

"Yes."

"Why were they here?"

"Complaining of malaise, qualmishness, and *mal de mer.*"

"Huh?"

Marge Supial bore down on me like the *Queen Mary* on an unlucky dinghy. "They felt sick to their little tum-tums," she said. "That's three questions; out you go!"

"But where did they—"

"Beat it!" she snarled.

Nurse Supial rushed me out the door. For a healer, she sure had a tough side. But was she capable of kidnapping? *Hmm.*

I mulled over her answers on the way back to class. Three bellyaches in a row, eh? Sounded like one of my parent-teacher conferences.

Mr. Ratnose looked up as I slipped into my seat.

"Well?" he asked. "Where's your note?"

"What note?"

My teacher's ears twitched. "The note from Nurse Supial about your sickness."

"Oh. She said it was all in my head."

Mr. Ratnose grimaced and turned back to the chalkboard. "Tell me something I don't know," he muttered.

9

Rookie Tookie Tavi

By the end of the day, I was regretting my bold undercover plan. What business did I have being on the football field?

Too fast, the clock's hands marched toward the last bell. My palms prickled. My stomach felt like last night's butterfly lasagna was making a break for it.

I was doomed.

The bell agreed. It rang a funeral dirge.

For once, I was the last student out the door. I cruised down the hall like the loser of a garden-snail drag race.

Coach Stroganoff and Jim Schortz were waiting in the gym—woodchuck and chuckwalla. All they needed to make three chucks was a chucklehead, and I knew who that was.

Me.

I gulped.

"Let's hustle, Gecko," said Coach. "Get dressed, and get out there!"

Jim walked me back to the equipment room. With his help, I strapped, snapped, and sealed myself into the uniform. It felt very natural, like angel wings on a warthog.

And it smelled nice, too. Whoever wore the uniform last had left behind enough B.O. to paralyze Paris.

I tried not to breathe.

The big chuckwalla thumped my shoulder pads. "Let's go, dude," said Jim.

We trundled along. I figured I might as well work on the case while waiting for my funeral.

"So, Jim," I said. "Tell me: Does Coach Stroganoff have any enemies?"

He stopped dead and stared. "What a weird thing to say. Why do you ask?"

I tugged at my slipping shoulder pads. "Uh, no particular reason. Just curious."

Jim Schortz gave a tight chuckle and smoothed his blue silk shirt. "No worries, dude," he said. "Coach is a great guy. Everybody likes him."

We started walking again.

"Wait," he said. "There *is* someone who's not too crazy about the coach."

"Who's that?"

Jim paused to slurp a grasshopper off a bush. Then he glanced around. "I probably shouldn't—*crunch*—say, but—*nulp*—Coach and the school nurse used to be sweet on each—*urp*—other. She felt bad when he dumped her."

I didn't feel that great myself, watching Jim's digestive process close-up.

"Would she try for revenge?" I asked.

He turned. "Hey, you mean like making those players disappear?" Jim Schortz wasn't quite the dim bulb I'd taken him for.

"Yeah, something like that," I said.

The chuckwalla smiled. "Dude, you're pretty good with this deduction stuff. Ever thought of getting into detective work?"

"You never know, Jimbo, you never know." I smirked.

Then we walked through the gate and into a sea of uniforms packed with mean, ugly football players. My smirk hung by one corner and dropped like a concrete kickball, right into my socks.

What was I thinking? The smallest of these guys was twice my size. Even the water boy was a hulk.

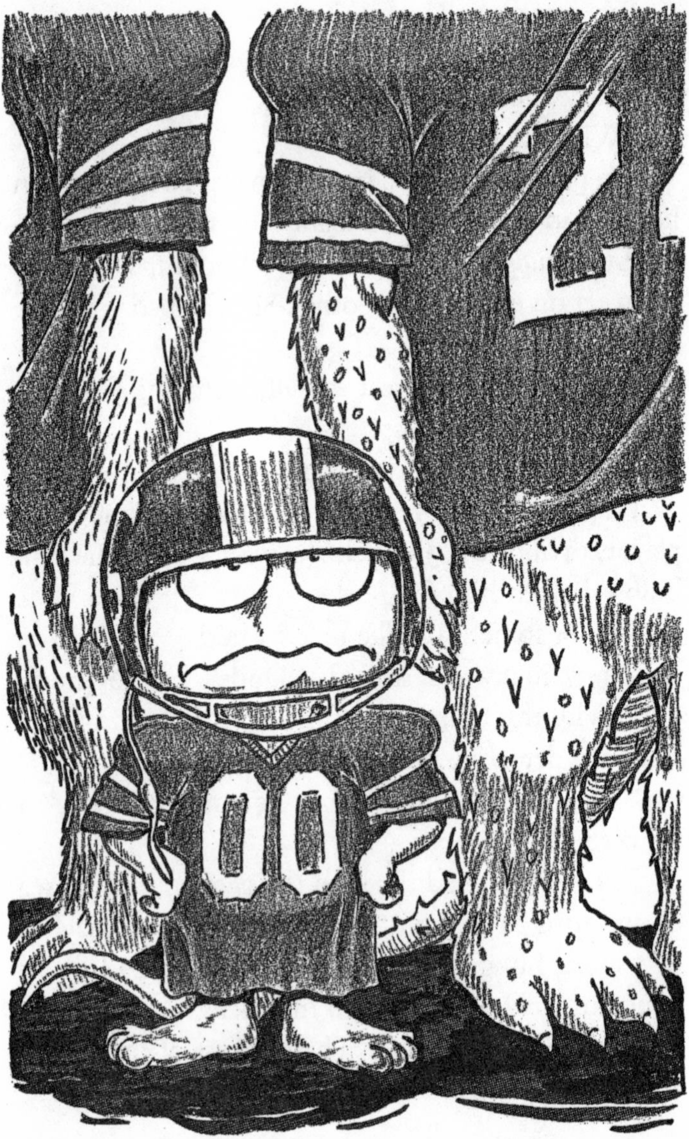

Coach Stroganoff plowed through the players and draped an arm, like a sleepy anaconda, over my shoulders. "Listen up, gentlemen."

"And women!" said one of the players, a hefty horned toad with painted-on eyelashes.

"Sorry, Queenie," Coach rumbled. "And women. As you know, we're a few players short, so I got us a new sub: Chet Gecko."

"Bit of a short player himself, isn't he?" a badger cracked.

The rest of the team chortled. I craned my neck and found many pairs of avid eyes under helmet visors—all watching me.

"Now, now," said the coach. "Treat him like one of your own."

Ah, that was nice of him.

"Fresh meat!" shouted Brick the hedgehog.

Or maybe not.

"Yaaahhh!" My new teammates piled on, pounding my helmet and shoulders, pumping my hands. The squirrel I'd seen outside the principal's office slapped my back hard enough to leave a paw print on my chest.

Coach's voice cut the hubbub like an ax through ice cream. "Enough mushy stuff, ladies."

"And gentlemen!" said the badger.

The coach *harrumph*ed. "Give me ten laps around the track and fifty push-ups."

The herd trompled off. I tried to dig my helmet out of my shoulder pads.

"Get the lead out, Gecko!" growled Coach Stroganoff.

"What, me, too?" I said.

"You, too, rookie." The titanic groundhog pointed the way with a sausage-like finger.

I trotted along after the other players, desperately hoping for a break in the case, or failing that, a stunt-man to handle my workout.

"Pick it up!" shouted the coach.

It was going to be a long, long day.

But sometimes, the case comes first—before pride, before common sense, before broken bones. That's the mark of a true detective.

Or a true moron, I forget which.

10

Bruised, Battered, and Bewildered

Two hours later, every muscle in my body hurt. My legs throbbed, my armpits ached, my tail felt like it'd been fed into a sausage grinder—even my tongue hurt. (Of course, maybe I should've tried catching the ball with my hands, instead.)

We'd undergone more forms of torture than I could count—running, blocking, speed drills, scrimmaging. Worst of all, I'd had no chance to snoop.

Of course, nothing suspicious happened. Maybe all the players didn't love one another. But they helped out when one blocker, a feisty crow, felt sick and went to the nurse.

The only bright spot was that Natalie had been right: Football players did get all the bubble gum they could chew. When Jim and the water boy passed it around, I packed my mouth full. My cheeks were bigger than the surly squirrel's (whose name, I learned, was P. Diddley).

When Coach Stroganoff blew that last whistle and the team trotted to the showers, I staggered to a bench and collapsed. All I wanted was a quick death.

A shadow with a long, pointy beak fell on the grass.

"Hey, hotshot, how was practice?" It was Natalie.

Too pooped to lift my head, I slurred, "Exercise should be against the law."

"Then only outlaws would exercise," she said.

"Suits me," I said. "Where you been?"

Natalie hopped onto the bench beside me, cheer-leader skirt swirling. "Practicing our cheers in the gym. We learned 'Fight, You Gophers, Fight'; 'Tunneling to Victory'; and 'Crush, Kill, Destroy.' How's the detecting?"

I told her about the love note I'd found in the nurse's office, and about Jim's tip that Nurse Supial and Coach Stroganoff had had a falling-out.

"You think she could be behind all this?" asked Natalie.

"It's a long shot, but we've got to check everything—even Coach's ex-girlfriends."

An unmistakably funky smell descended on us with the subtlety of a Force 5 hurricane.

"Whew!" said Natalie. "Who cut the—"

"Gecko and birdie," sneered Herman the Gila Monster. "Big-time detectives."

I looked up. "Herman."

My client might not have been the sharpest pencil in the pocket protector, but at least he hadn't blown my cover during practice. Aside from the occasional, bone-shattering block, he hadn't spoken to me. I soon learned why.

"You big-time liar," he said.

"I never lie," I said.

That wasn't strictly true. I *had* lied before, but not to Herman—at least not recently.

"You say you like help, but you like play football," he said. "You lie."

I swayed to my feet and held out my hands. "Relax, big guy," I said. "I didn't *want* to join the team."

Natalie jumped in. "That's right. Chet's gone undercover. He's just pretending to play."

The Gila monster picked me up by my helmet. I looked straight into his bloodshot eyeballs.

"Find players fast," he said, "if you know what good for you."

"Long naps, healthy food, and plenty of playtime," I said. "But what's that got to do with anything?"

Foomp!

Herman dropped me like a rancid sandwich and stomped off to the showers.

Natalie shook her head. "You sure can smooth talk a client," she said.

I moaned. "Help me up."

"You want up? This'll cheer you up: Why did the doughnut maker retire?" She grinned at me, waiting.

I grunted.

"Because he was fed up with the hole business." Natalie cackled.

I muttered, "I know how he feels."

After a shower and a change, I limped out of the gym. Hard to believe that some kids actually *volunteered* to get beat up like this.

Natalie was leaning against a wall, chatting with Frenchy LaTrine, the mousy cheerleader.

"Hiii, Chet!" called Frenchy.

"What pom-pom did you crawl out of?" I gave her my steely look.

Natalie waved me over. "Frenchy was just saying something interesting."

I joined them. "Spill it, Frenchy."

She spilled. It seemed that a guy she knew, Buford the skunk, was a wanna-be football player.

"He's not strong like you, Chet—he didn't make

the team!" said Frenchy. "Poor guy—now he's always Mr. Grumpy Face. I told him, turn that frown upside down!"

"And did he?" asked Natalie.

"No way, Jose!" said Frenchy. "But he did agree to be water boy! That's a start, isn't it?"

It was indeed. But not in the way she thought.

If anybody held a grudge against the team, it'd be someone jealous—someone like Buford. That skunk bore watching.

I grunted my thanks. My wobbly legs carried me homeward.

"See you later, Chet?" called Frenchy.

"Yeah," I said. "The later, the better."

This case held more danger than I'd first suspected. Not only would my client knock my block off if I failed, but the investigation carried another risk: cheerleaders.

And between a butt-whomping and a snootful of cooties, I'd choose the butt-whomping every time.

11

Hickory, Dickory, Jock

Whether or not you're a bird, every school has its pecking order. The jocks beat up the brains, the brains pick on the oddballs, and the bullies bother everybody.

Somehow, the word had gotten out overnight: Chet Gecko was now a jock.

When I limped into school the next day, students treated me differently. The guys gave me more respect, and the dames—well, let's just say they were more obnoxious than before.

It didn't float my boat. After yesterday's workout, I felt like leftovers from a vulture's lunch pail.

At recess, my sore feet led me toward the sixth graders' playground.

Halfway there, they were joined by a pair of birdie claws belonging to Natalie Attired. "Hiya, Chet!" she said. "You're sure draggin' your wagon today."

"*Mmf,*" I grunted. I'm always quick with a comeback.

"You know, if you plan to stay on the team, you really oughta get in shape."

"I am in shape," I said. "Round is a shape."

Natalie smirked. "So, where we headed?"

I raised a limp arm to point. "To the sixth graders' stomping grounds," I said. "We need answers. My body can't take much more undercover work."

A bunch of football players (a huddle? a thickness?) were standing under the trees, acting mature. I could tell because they were pulling girls' tails, punching one another's shoulders, and giving wedgies to weaker guys.

My teammates, love 'em or leave 'em.

I planned to leave them as soon as possible.

Natalie and I approached. Besides Justin Case (our otter quarterback), I noticed P. Diddley, Queenie the horned toad, and Brick the hedgehog.

"Hey, sports fans," I said. "What's shakin'?"

Queenie chuckled. "Your knees, rookie," she rasped. "You were so lame at yesterday's practice."

The others hooted.

"Don't hold back, Queenie," I said. "Tell me what you *really* think."

She took a breath. "You were lamer than a—"

"Thanks, I get the idea." Sarcasm is wasted on horned toads.

Natalie tried for small talk. "So, how we gonna do in the big game?"

"Who dis?" said P. Diddley.

My partner threw out her wings in a frightening display. "Gimme an *N*, gimme an *A*, gimme a *T-A*—"

"A cheerleader," I said, punching her lightly. "She's with me."

"*Ow.*" Natalie rubbed her shoulder.

Queenie grinned. She liked pain—as long as it was someone else's.

Brick scratched his neck bristles. "The big game doesn't look good," he said. "We lost some key players."

"Yeah," said Justin, stretching his passing arm. "And we're scraping the bottom of the barrel for replacements." He nodded at me. "No offense."

"None taken," I said. "So where do you think those missing guys went?"

P. Diddley spat between his buckteeth. "Sumpin' happened, sumpin' bad."

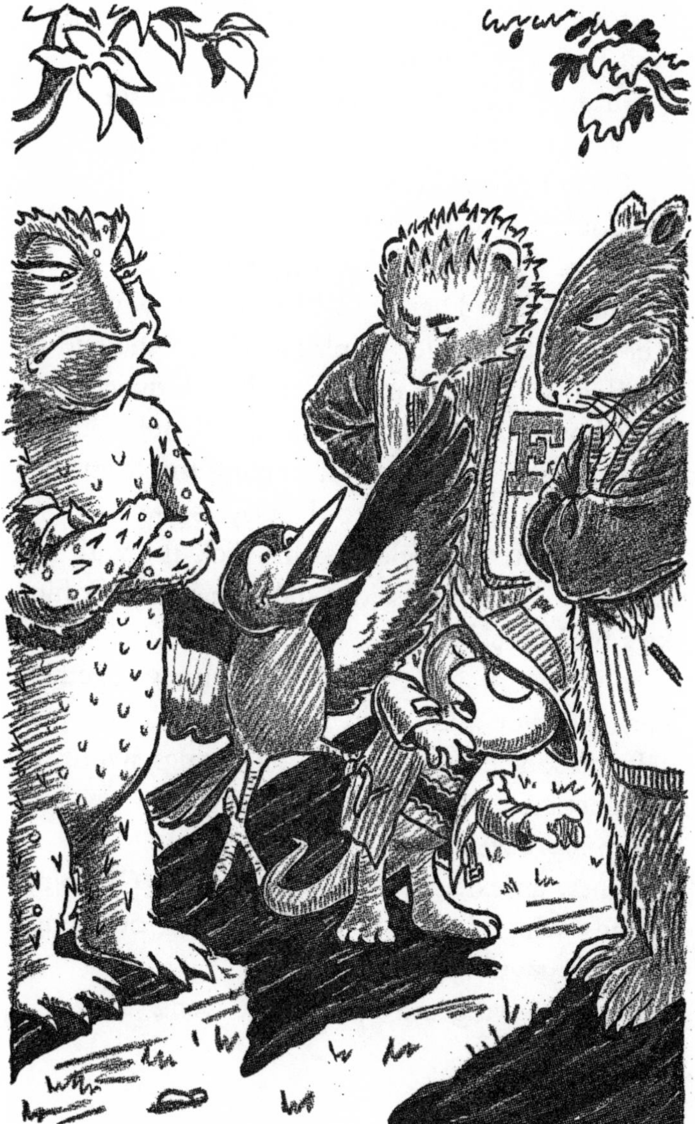
F

I took a different tack. "What do you guys think about Buford, the water boy?"

Queenie cracked her knuckles. "That loser? Why you wanna know?"

"I heard he tried to make the team."

"Couldn't cut da mustard," said P. Diddley. He spat again.

Natalie cocked her head. "I didn't know you had to be a mustard cutter to play football," she said to me. "Do you have to make a pigskin sandwich?"

I elbowed her and asked Justin, "Could Buford be so cheesed off about not making the team that he'd do something awful to the players?"

The quarterback cleaned his slick fur with his tongue. "Buford?" he said. "Hah! They'd break him like a bread stick."

Suspicion drew P. Diddley's features together. "Hey, why you askin' all dees questions?"

In unison, my teammates' ugly mugs swung in my direction.

Rrrrinngg! went the bell.

I knew an exit cue when I heard one. Grabbing Natalie's wing, I said, "They're playing our song. Gotta go, guys."

And on a wing and a prayer, we went.

12

Beefie Baby

I don't care what anyone says, cafeteria food is one of the joys of school. Where else can you get baked beans and greasy horsefly burritos without having to sweet-talk your mom?

Natalie and I found a relatively quiet bench in the lunchroom and sat down for our south-of-the-border delight. When the last cheesy fly had been munched, we hit the doors—fed and feisty and looking for suspects.

First on the list was Marge Supial, ex-girlfriend and grumpy nurse.

Two minutes and a short crawl through the bushes later, we peeked into Nurse Supial's window. No patients waited. No business pressed. It was slower than the last lap of a glacier race in her office.

The wombat sat at her desk, head drooping in the first stages of a nap attack.

I nodded to Natalie. She made a sound like the static of an intercom. *Kzztch!*

Mockingbirds. They sure can mock.

"Nurse Supial?" said Natalie in Coach Stroganoff's voice. "Marge?"

Her gray-furred head snapped up. "Beefie?"

Beefie? I mouthed. Natalie and I barely stifled our giggles. We dived for cover.

"Are you all right?" asked the nurse, addressing the intercom.

"Uh, yes," said Natalie. "Had something in my throat. Marge, I must ask you something..."

"Oh, yes, my love muffin, all is forgiven."

I made a face at Natalie. *Love muffin?* This wombat had it bad.

"Um, that's nice," said Natalie-as-Coach. "Tell me, did Tito the crow come in yesterday feeling sick?"

"Well, uh, he did," said the nurse.

"And where did he go afterward?" asked Natalie.

I risked a quick peek through the window. Nurse Supial was leaning over her intercom with a puzzled frown on her furry mug. I sank down again.

"I treated his stomachache and sent the lad off with Mr. Schortz," she said. "Didn't Mr. Schortz call the boy's parents to pick him up?"

Natalie went wide-eyed. "Oh, uh . . ."

I glared at her, and she recovered. "I, er, haven't seen Jim today," she said, continuing her Coach Stroganoff impression.

"Is everything okay?" said the nurse. "You sound funny."

"Just this darn Chet cold—I mean, chest cold," Natalie said.

I gave Natalie the OK sign and peeked in at the nurse again.

"Alrighty, then," said Natalie. "Gotta go."

"But, love muffin, what about us?" Nurse Supial pouted.

"Uh, we'll always have Paris."

"Oh, Beefie, I knew you wouldn't forget!" said the wombat.

"Adoo, ma cherry!" said Natalie. *"Kzztch!"*

"What?" I whispered to my partner, ducking out of sight.

As we crawled out of the bushes, she explained, "I saw that in one of my sister's soap operas. It's romantic."

"It's weird," I said. "But nice Stroganoff impression, Beefie Baby."

We strolled down the hall. Natalie groomed her feathers. "So," she said, "do you believe Nurse Supial is involved?"

"Not with the kidnapping, if that's what you mean."

Natalie cocked her head. "So we scratch one suspect."

"But there's another one we haven't scratched," I said. "Buford the skunk."

"Uh, if you don't mind, Chet," said Natalie. "You scratch him."

13

Punk Skunk

We didn't have to search long. On a low wall at the edge of the grass squatted Buford the skunk, our team's water boy. His tail drooped. His matted black-and-white fur looked as soggy as a plumber's hanky.

If Buford was a scientist, he'd be the guy who invented the Bummer-tron.

"Hey, water boy," I said. "How's tricks?"

His muddy brown eyes gave us the once-over. "I owe ya money, or what?" he asked.

"We just want to talk," said Natalie. "I'm the new cheerleader, Natalie Attired, and this is Che—"

"I know who he is," sneered the skunk. "Mr. Hotshot Football Player, Mr. No-need-to-try-out,

Mr. I'm-so-cool-I-can-make-the-team-in-fourth-grade."

Call it a crazy hunch, but something told me Buford didn't like me. That was okay. I'd handled plenty of tough subjects before (especially if you count math and spelling).

"Relax, buddy boy," I said. "After all, we're on the same team."

Buford shot me a look that could've fried mothcakes without a griddle. "You mean, *you're* on the team. I just carry the water."

"And a darn good job you're doing," said Natalie. "I think you're the best water boy this team's ever had."

Her flattery rolled off him like spit off a frog's fanny.

"Gee, thanks," he said. "That's like being the best moron."

The phrase *If the shoe fits...* crossed my mind, but I kept it to myself. I squatted beside Buford. "I'm just curious about my teammates. Thought maybe you'd know, since you're in the thick of things."

The desire to scorn me and the need to show off fought behind Buford's eyes. Pride won. The skunk wiped his runny nose with a grubby paw.

"Shoot," he said. "I could tell ya a lot—if I wanted to."

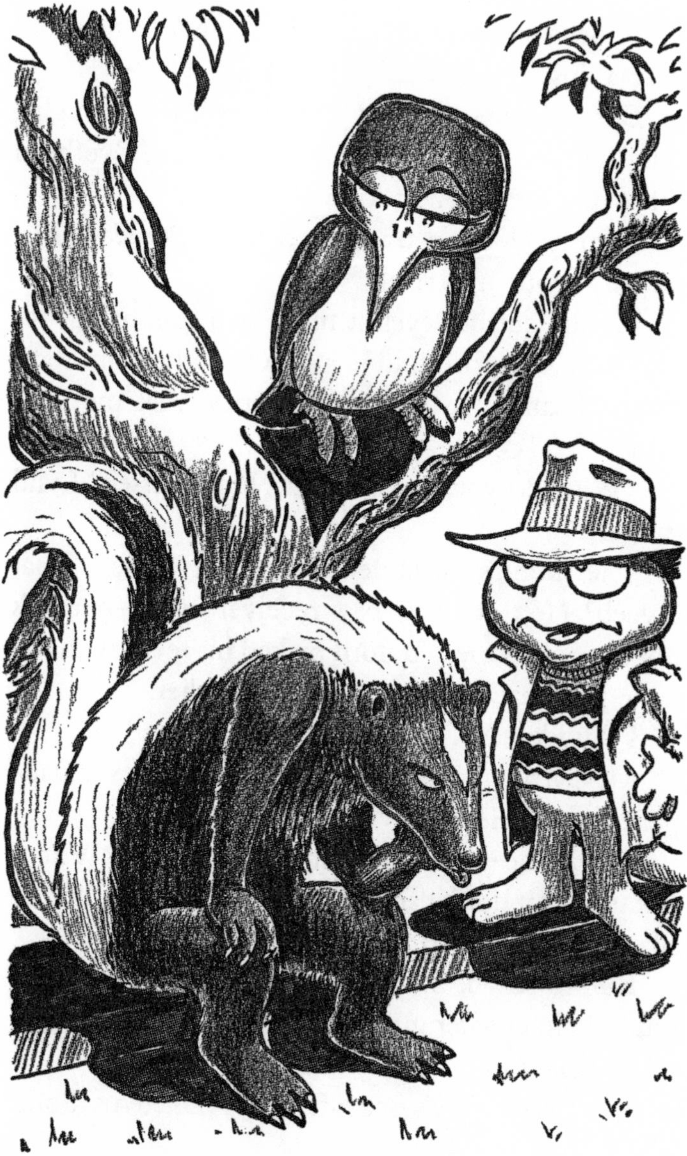

"I bet you know all about the team's history and everything," said Natalie.

Buford's chest swelled. "Sure do. Even though I only transferred from Petsadena this year, I've been following the Gophers for a while."

I frowned. He'd transferred from *Petsadena Elementary*—our arch rival?

Natalie cut her eyes at me. She'd caught it, too.

"Yeah," Buford told her, "I know the team stats, most valuable players—all that stuff. Ask me anything."

"What do you know about Hugh Geste?" I said casually.

The skunk's lip curled. He told Natalie, "That dweeb? He's our best pass receiver ever—but he's not as good as me." Buford picked his teeth with the same paw that had wiped his nose earlier.

I shuddered.

My partner picked up the ball. "Whatever happened to ol' Hugh, anyway?"

"Well, he—" The skunk broke off. "Wait a minute. You don't care about the team at all. You're sweet on that stupid football player."

Buford stood. Suspicion darkened his face like a mud pie in a water glass.

"What? No way," said Natalie.

The water boy's scornful gaze raked us both.

"Dunno why I'm wasting my time with you two losers." He spun on his heel and slouched off.

Natalie watched him go. "As the worm said when her husband disappeared, what's eating him?"

"The green-eyed monster," I said.

Natalie frowned. "You mean Herman's older brother?"

"No, featherhead. Jealousy."

"Ah." She smiled. "He wants *on* that team as bad as you want *off* it."

I started walking. "And he can have my spot. Just as soon as we've solved this case."

Natalie and I ambled across the playground. "Do you think Buford could be a double agent for Pets-adena?" she asked.

"He'd have a hard time being a *single* agent," I said. "But anything's possible."

Natalie grinned. "Anything? How about you acing your next science test?"

"Well," I said, "*almost* anything."

14

Have Gum, Will Travel

The rest of the school day was nothing to write home about. (Actually, they never are—except at report card time.) I did my schoolwork, I kept my mouth shut, I waited for the last bell.

When it rang, I headed for the gymnasium. If the only way off the football team was to solve the case, I had to get crackin' before my head got cracked.

All padded and helmeted, I joined the rest of the gorillas—I mean, my teammates—on the benches at the edge of the field. They were slurping sports drinks and practicing operatic belches. Classy.

Stripy tail dragging, Buford walked down the line, passing out bubble gum. As he reached me, the skunk shoved a stick in my face. "Bite this!" he grumped.

I took the gum, inspected it carefully for boogers, then slipped it into my mouth. My tongue danced with a butterscotchy flavor. *Mmm,* pond slug.

A burning gaze prickled my neck, and I turned. From halfway down the bench, Herman's electric stare bored into me. He didn't speak, but I could feel his question: *Well . . . ?*

Coach Stroganoff paced the grass before us, Jim Schortz trailing him like a scaly shadow. The players fell silent under our leader's gimlet-eyed gaze.

"In just two days," he said, "we face the Petsadena Baboons. I don't have to tell you, we're in a tight spot."

"Tight spot," echoed Jim.

"We're missing key players, including Tito the crow . . ."

The crow who got sick at yesterday's practice! I searched Buford's face for a reaction, but his sneer looked like it'd been carved on.

Coach continued, "And our win-loss record is atrocious."

"Expi-ali-docious," said Jim Schortz.

The coach glanced at the chuckwalla, who shrugged. The groundhog thrust his jaw forward. "We need to come up with something special to beat them."

"Special, 'kay," said Jim.

I braced myself for the big pep talk.

Coach paused to regard each of us in turn. "And so, to build team spirit, everyone gets...a nickname."

"Nickname?" I muttered, glancing up at the quarterback, Justin. He rolled his eyes.

Jim Schortz wheeled up a chalkboard. On the left half were the months of the year, each followed by an adjective, like *mad, deranged, mutant,* or *warped.* On the right side were the letters of the alphabet followed by nouns, like *monster, washing machine, barbecue,* and *bugmuncher.*

Mr. Ratnose would've been pleased that I recognized nouns and adjectives. I don't know what he would've thought about the coach's list.

Beef Stroganoff grabbed a pointer and waved it at the board. "Find your birth month," he said, "for the first half of your name..."

We dutifully found our months.

"Then add the word beside the first letter of your last name. Put 'em together, and that's your new nickname!"

Several football players asked for help in spelling their last names. Others weren't sure which month they were born. But eventually we all sorted it out.

"What's your nickname?" I asked Justin.

"Angry Hairdryer," he said. "Yours?"

I made a face. "Stinky Bottomchucker."

He snorted. "Oh, yeah. That'll scare our enemies."

The team spirit was so thick you could barely breathe—especially if you were cackling at someone else's nickname (Lumpy Toaster and Deranged Bugmuncher, for example).

We giggled all the way through the rundown of that day's plays. Coach Stroganoff's bristly eyebrows lowered like two caterpillars settling down for a nap.

"Ten laps, right now!" he growled.

Ten times around the track cut down on the giggle factor. In fact, it cut down on the breathing. By the end, I was sucking wind like a jumbo vacuum cleaner.

My teammates trotted onto the field for scrimmage. I bent over with hands on knees.

"Oooh."

Exhaustion brought on hallucinations. I swore I could hear my own moans, and I wasn't making a sound (aside from panting).

"Oooh-ugh."

My head swiveled sideways. There stood Justin Case, star quarterback and stud otter, grabbing his furry belly.

I gasped, "What's wrong... Angry Hairdryer?"

He folded in half. "I—*ooogh*—don't feel so good."

The assistant coach spotted us and hustled over,

wattles shaking. "What's happening, Funky Bottom-biter?" he asked me.

I pointed at myself. "Stinky Bottomchucker." I jerked a thumb at Justin. "Sick Quarterbacker."

Jim's eyes went wide. He guided the ailing otter past the other players and through the arriving cheerleaders. I straightened to watch them go.

Jim and Justin weaved right by the water boy, Buford. The skunk flashed a little smile as they passed.

What was going on *there*?

I knew I'd have to figure it out later.

How did I know? Call it that keen detective sense.

Or call it a football shoved into my gut and a coach's voice booming, "Let's play some ball!"

15

Polecat in the Hat

Our practice session was fun. If you like over-sized freaks with strange nicknames playing bumper cars with your body. And it was as relaxing as a long nap inside a cement mixer.

The cheerleaders practiced their routines in between gawking at the football players. My teammates showed off. Disgusting.

At long last, Coach blew his whistle, ending our torment. "Hit the showers!" he cried. I hit the bench to rest up for the trip while the other players jogged off.

"Not you, mister!" shouted Coach Stroganoff. He flagged down Herman the Gila Monster and pulled him aside.

Feeling snoopy, I scooted down the bench to listen. Neither of them noticed.

"Expected to see those missing players by now," the brawny groundhog was saying as I came within earshot. "Well?"

The Gila monster glowered. "Not my fault," he said. "Someone helping me—he slow."

The coach planted a fist on his hip. "Don't feed me that malarkey, buster. You've got one more day."

Herman pouted. "Okay, Coach." Then he rubbed his gut. "*Oogh.* Sore."

Coach Stroganoff raised an eyebrow. "Oh, you see Justin get sick, and you think you can act sick for sympathy?" he asked. "No dice. Bring those missing guys tomorrow, or you're off the team."

Herman trudged off, still rubbing his belly.

The coach clomped over to the bleachers to consult with Jim Schortz.

I scanned the field. On the sidelines, the cheerleaders were finishing their practice and packing up their pom-poms. I shuddered. They had enough concentrated cooties to power the Space Shuttle of Love.

Near the far fence, Buford the skunk was chatting with an older polecat in a pillbox hat. She patted his shoulder and he jerked away.

I watched our water boy as cheerleaders crossed the field. What was his game, anyway?

Suddenly a pair of paws clamped over my eyes and the world went dark. "Guess who?" a girl's voice asked.

"Typhoid Mary?" I said.

"No, guess again!"

"Someone who's about to lose a finger?" I reached for the paws.

"No, silly! It's me!" She let go. I turned to see Frenchy LaTrine, the mousy cheerleader. "Waiting for me?" she asked.

"Dream on." I jerked a thumb at Buford. "I was watching him. Hey, who's he talking to?"

Frenchy's long nose wrinkled as she squinted at the critter. "Not exactly sure," she said. "I think she's a football mom. She's been here before."

Hmm. Had the polecat been spying on our practice? Was she working hand-in-stinky-glove with Buford the skunk?

"Thanks, Frenchy," I said. "You're all right, for a rodent."

She ducked her head. "Thanks!"

I swayed to my feet and hobbled to the showers.

Halfway there, Natalie turned up. "Lots of sickos out there today," she said.

"You gotta be pretty sick to play this sport."

"Not that kind of sicko, Chet. I meant Justin and Herman."

I took off my helmet and tucked it under my arm. "Justin was sick; I think our client was just faking."

"Something's fishy here," she said, waving a wing.

"I'll take a shower," I said.

Natalie shook her head. "Not that kind of fishy. Think about it, Chet: First, Hugh, Lou, and Dewey get sick..."

I picked it up. "Then, Tito the crow..."

"And now, Justin and maybe Herman." She grabbed my arm. "I think whoever's behind the kidnappings is slipping something to the players that makes them sick."

I stopped. "Of course!" I said. "But what? It's not the gum."

"Why not?"

"I've had it for two days, and I'm fine."

Natalie smirked. "So?" she said. "You once ate a whole colony of chocolate-covered ants and didn't even burp."

I pointed a finger. "Yeah, but what about the other players? Everybody chews gum, but they only get sick one at a time."

"*Hmm*...you're right." Natalie paced. "What about those sports drinks?"

"Same thing. Everyone drinks 'em."

My partner stopped and cocked her head. "So if somebody's doctoring food or drink..."

The light went on in the fridge of my brain. "It'd have to be someone with access," I said. "Someone like..."

Our eyes met. "Buford," we said together.

"That skunk," said Natalie.

"You said it. And we've only got one more day to shut down his plot."

She looked puzzled. "Why's that?"

"Because if we don't do it by tomorrow's practice, Herman will shut *me* down."

Natalie shivered. "Ah."

"And what's worse, he won't give us any cake."

She looked at me closely. "Chet?"

"Yeah?"

"We've got to have a talk about your priorities."

16

Phone Vivant

There's something to be said for spending your morning in the pursuit of knowledge. What that is, I don't know.

The next day, I spent my morning running different scenarios on the jock kidnappings. Nothing quite clicked.

If Buford was our bad guy, how was he working his scheme? Did he have an accomplice—maybe that football mom? But what was her motivation?

This case had more angles than a pile of polygons. (And Mr. Ratnose says I don't pay attention in geometry.)

At first recess, Natalie and I checked around for Justin Case and Herman the Gila Monster. No luck.

We did find Queenie, who told us that neither player had shown up for school today.

I won't say time flew (it limped), but eventually the clock rolled around to lunchtime. The bell set me free to pursue my two favorite things: food and detective work.

Mrs. Bagoong and her lunch crew had outdone themselves that day—dwarf spiders au gratin, sweet potatoes, and county fair fireflies. I was picking my teeth with a spider leg when Natalie leaned across the lunch table.

"Now can we go?" she asked.

I belched gently. "Now we can go."

But the question was, *Where to go?*

Lacking a better plan, Natalie and I searched the school for the missing football players. I didn't think we'd find them, and I wasn't disappointed. They were better hidden than a snake's belly button.

We gave up. Around us, kids and teachers followed their usual kid-ly and teacher-ly activities. It was a normal school day, like nothing had changed.

"Wait a minute," I said. "Something doesn't add up here."

"Your math homework?" Natalie asked.

"Besides that. These football players have been missing for days—a week, some of them."

"True..."

"Don't you think it's weird that nobody's freaking out?"

Natalie fluffed her feathers. "Besides Herman and the coach, you mean?"

"Exactly," I said. "Why hasn't someone called the cops?"

Natalie polished her beak on a shoulder. "But Herman said that Coach Stroganoff had phoned their parents."

I snapped my fingers. "What if he was wrong?" I said.

We hotfooted it for the pay phones while I searched my pockets for Hugh's school record. I found it wrapped around a slightly squashed, half-eaten millipede sandwich.

Thank goodness for sloppy housekeeping.

"You're on," I said, passing the damp paper to my partner.

Natalie dialed Hugh's parents while I finished off the sandwich. No sense in wasting good food. She twisted the phone receiver so we both could hear.

A man's voice answered. "Hello, Geste residence."

"Uh, hi, this is Mrs. Crow from your kid's—I mean, your son's school," said Natalie in a fair imitation of the school secretary.

"Ask where Hugh is," I whispered to Natalie.

"What?" asked the voice.

"What?" asked Natalie.

"Where's Hugh?" I hissed, as loud as I dared.

"Gesundheit," said the fake Mrs. Crow. Into the phone, Natalie added, "Someone sneezed."

"Oh," said the voice. "How may I help you?"

I didn't dare whisper again, so I just waved my hands at Natalie. Being a bird, she winged it.

"Oh, yes," she said. "We're, uh, having a hard time finding your son?"

I pressed my ear to the phone for Hugh's father's reaction. It surprised me.

He chuckled. "Don't you school employees talk to each other? We got a call last week from his coach, said that Hugh would be off at football camp through tomorrow."

Natalie's eyes went wide. *"Football camp?"* she repeated, her accent slipping.

"Hey," said Hugh's father. "Who is this, really?"

Oops. I wrestled the receiver toward me. "Hi, is John there?" I asked.

"There's no John here," the voice replied.

"Then where do you go to the bathroom?" I giggled falsely.

A grunt of disgust came from the phone. "Crazy kids!" he shouted.

I hung up. Natalie and I stared at each other, as perplexed as two penguins in a pomegranate tree.

She scratched her head. "How could he be at football camp without the coach knowing it?" she said.

"I don't know. But it's time to get some answers . . . straight from the groundhog's mouth."

"All right," said Natalie. "I just hope he flosses regularly."

17

Gym Dandy

The gym's double doors stood open like a giant's gap-toothed smile. We breezed past some kids playing basketball and crossed to the coach's office.

Assistant Coach Jim Schortz sat licking his fingers, with his feet up on his boss's desk and an empty lunch tray before him.

"Whassup, dude?" he said.

"Where's Coach Stroganoff?" I asked.

He scratched his throat wattles. "Dunno," he said. "Running errands?"

Natalie pushed up against the desk. "Maybe you can help us," she cooed.

"I'll sure try," he said. Jim grinned and put his hands behind his head, flexing his biceps in turn. His silk jumpsuit stretched.

I doubted the big muscle-headed dandy could help us find the gym door if his tail was shut in it. Still, he was the assistant coach.

"It's like this," I said. "Herman told us that Coach had called the missing kids' parents, and they said their kids weren't at home—"

Natalie interrupted. "But we just called Hugh's dad, and he said Hugh has been off at football camp since last week. Something screwy's going on."

Jim's mouth fell open. He looked from Natalie to me. "No way," he said.

"Yes, way," I answered.

Natalie checked the open doorway behind us for eavesdroppers. "Someone's kidnapped these guys and is trying to cover it up."

"Who do you suspect?" he asked.

Mr. Ratnose would've told him it's *whom* do you suspect, but I never gave two hoots for grammar. I leaned back on my tail. "We're not sure. But it could be the water boy."

The chuckwalla's eyes widened. "Buford," he said. "Of course! He's the one, dude. Have you told anyone else?"

I shook my head. "Nobody. Our client is, uh, laying low, and Coach thinks I'm just a football player."

"Aren't you?" asked Jim.

"We're really private eyes," said Natalie. "But nobody on the team knows."

"Let's keep it that way," said Jim.

"Why?" I asked.

The chuckwalla lowered his voice. "Coach has a lot on his mind with the big game coming up tomorrow. It'd be a feather in my cap if I find these kids."

If he finds them? Pssh. Everybody wants to be a detective.

"Well, I . . . ," I said.

Natalie touched her wing tip to his arm. "It'll be our secret."

Jim's eyes flicked to me.

"Yeah, sure, why not," I said. A thought struck me. "Hey, maybe you *can* do something. You know that polecat who talks to Buford after practice?"

He nodded.

"Who is she?"

"Dunno her name," said Jim, "but she's from Petsadena." His eyes lit up. "Say, you don't think . . . ?"

"That she's in cahoots with Buford?" said Natalie. "Absolutely."

Jim Schortz tossed a baseball. "Wow, dudes, this is exciting."

"Isn't it?" I said. "See what you can dig up on Mrs. Petsadena, and we'll cover Buford."

"Deal," he said. "And remember,"—Jim put a clawed finger to his lips—"dumb's the word."

"Dumb and dumber," I agreed.

Truer words were never spoken. Jim was so dumb, if you gave him a penny for his thoughts, you'd get change.

18

In Hog We Trust

Our last football practice was as jolly as Christmas Eve in Dracula's castle. We barely had enough players to make up a team.

Lining the bench to either side of me were some of the longest faces you'd ever see outside of an anteaters' convention.

Everyone knew we were going to get creamed in tomorrow's game.

Everyone but the coach, that is.

The huge groundhog paced before us, reading football wisdom from *The Little Red Book of Football Wisdom* by Coach Dumbrowski.

Even that comic relief didn't help.

"If at first down, you don't succeed, hike, hike

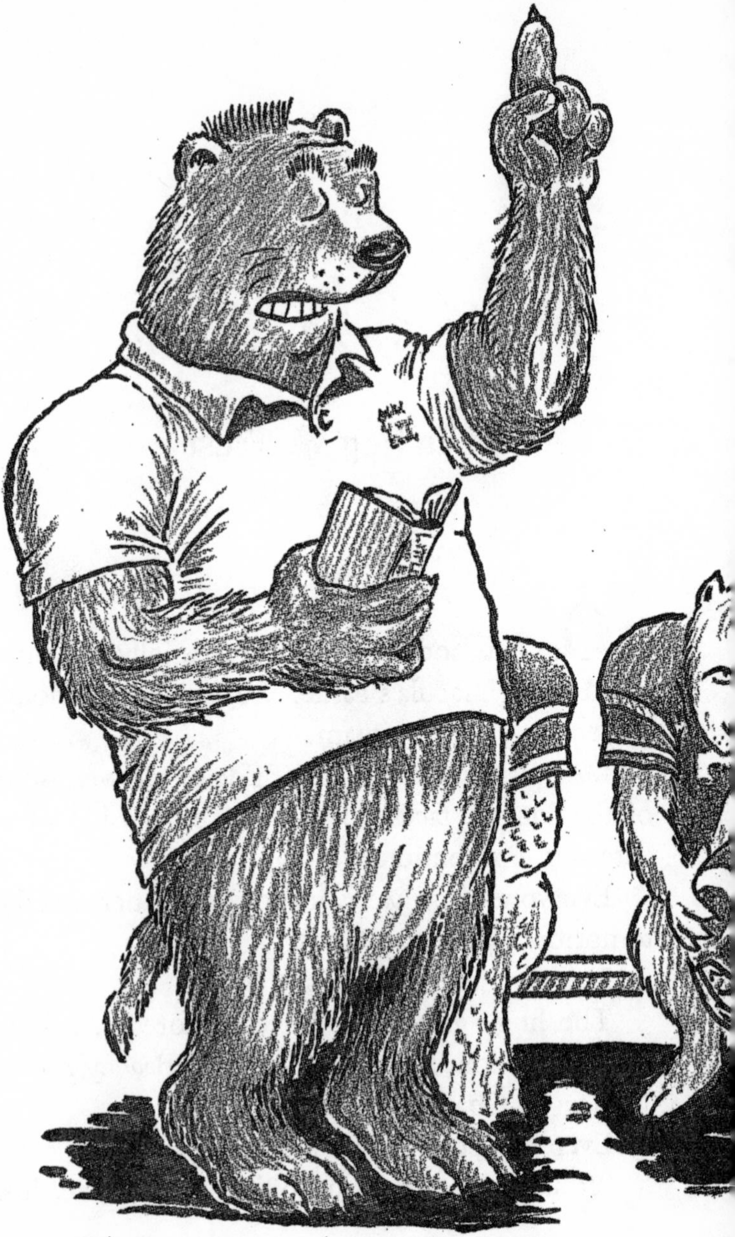

again," Coach Stroganoff read. "Too many quarter-backs . . . spoil the huddle."

The pep talk ground on and on, until the pep was flatter than yesterday's pop. Over by the bleachers, the cheerleaders began practicing their routines. Natalie gave me a thumbs-up—she was on the lookout.

Finally, Coach sent us onto the field.

"And remember," he shouted. "Use those nick-names!"

All the time I was trying to catch passes from Twisted Blowdryer (or was he Mad Refrigerator?) I kept an eye on our water boy, Buford.

This wasn't easy. Several times I tripped over my tail or ran out-of-bounds. (Fortunately, most of the players played that badly, so nobody noticed.)

Here's what I saw: Buford sulking on the sidelines; Buford pulling sports drinks from the cooler; Buford picking his nose.

None of this seemed especially sinister, but I didn't give up hope. Before long, Natalie or I would catch him in the act.

By the end of practice, with the skunk behaving like a model water boy, nobody had gotten sick. Then I suspected the truth: He was on to us. Either Buford had good radar, or someone had tipped him off.

As I started for the showers, I gave our water boy a hard stare. He returned his usual glum-and-surly look—no *nyah-nyah*, no *I-sure-tricked-you*.

I couldn't beat a confession out of him; this was one big skunk. But maybe I could trick him. . . .

"Hey, Buford," I said. "What's shakin'?"

He glowered down at me. "Whaddaya want?"

"A word."

"How about *moron*?"

"It suits you," I said. "Tell me, what do you think of our chances tomorrow?"

Buford's lip curled. "Without all our best guys?" he said. "Slim and none."

I removed my helmet, the better to study his face. "Bet that makes you happy, being from Petsadena and all."

Buford's tail raised. His expression was colder than a polar bear's earwax. "Is that what ya bet? You'd lose, Gecko."

Something off to one side caught Buford's eye. I followed his gaze. Over by the fence stood the little old polecat from Petsadena, carrying a paper sack and waving.

"Better get over there and meet your contact," I said. "Has she got the stomachache pills in that bag?"

"What—" His comeback faded as we watched Jim Schortz hustle up to the polecat.

"Who is that lady?" I asked.

"She's—just someone I know," said the skunk, looking past me.

"What's she want with you?" I moved to block him.

He glanced at me, then back to the pair in the parking lot. "She's my ride, okay? Like it's any of your business."

I crossed my arms. "You expect me to believe that?"

"Believe it or not," he said. "She, uh, works at the pharmacy in town."

I risked a quick peek over my shoulder. The polecat was running away from Jim.

"Gotta go," said Buford. He pushed past me and trucked off after her.

I sat on the bench and waited for the cheerleaders to finish. It didn't take long. Natalie flapped across the field and landed on the bench beside me.

"Did you get a load of that?" she said.

"Yup. Looks like your friend Jim put a scare into her."

I told her what I'd learned from Buford about the Petsadena mom working in the pharmacy.

Natalie hopped in excitement. "That's great, Chet! Now we know where Buford got his poison pills."

"But we still don't understand how he made the players disappear." I scratched my head. "You know, maybe we've been going about this all wrong."

"What do you mean?" asked Natalie.

"Maybe we should give up trying to figure out *how,* and concentrate on *where*—where to find those missing players."

Natalie cocked her head. "Well, we didn't find them at Emerson Hicky," she said. "So I have a hunch the answers are at Petsadena."

"Partner, I have a hunch your hunch is right."

"Thanks. I have a hunch your hunch about my hunch is right."

"And I have a hunch your—ah, never mind."

19

Countdown to Injury

Friday morning dawned cool and crisp as a frozen Pillbug Crunch bar. And the day brought with it some good news. After punishing my body with a week of killer workouts, I didn't feel the pain anymore.

I was testing my newfound fitness on the swing set.

"Hey, Natalie," I said, pushing off. "My muscles aren't sore. Does this mean I'm getting in shape?"

She eyeballed me from the next swing over. "Nope," she said, as I slipped off the swing and fell to the sand. "You're numb."

Ah, the benefits of exercise.

I climbed back on. We swung in silence for a while. Carefully. It was recess—school's reward for staying awake a couple of hours.

Around us, students simmered with excitement over the game. Kids wore badges that read BASH THE BABOONS! (Petsadena's mascot), and they kept coming up to me saying things like "Attaboy!" and "Go, Gophers!"

The day passed in a haze of football spirit and foolishness. Somehow, I made it to last period.

In Mr. Ratnose's class, it was "free reading time." This meant we could read anything we wanted to— except for comic books, gory tales, and stories the PTA didn't like. (In short, most of the fun stuff.)

I slumped in my seat with a copy of *Stewart, Belittled* open before me. I mused. Maybe the answers to my case lay at Petsadena, but I wasn't looking forward to going there. I wondered, *Would I come back in one piece?*

After the last bell rang, the halls were hopping like grasshoppers on a griddle. Kids flowed toward the parking lot, where buses and cars idled, waiting to take them to the big game.

Beside the gym, my own chariot stood: a dirt-brown bus for the players, staff, and cheerleaders. The school mascot, a golden gopher, leered down from its painted side.

"Hey, check this out, Gecko!" called Brick, lounging by the door. He laughed and hooked a thumb toward the front of the rig.

Across the grill, some wit had strapped a dummy of Petsadena's baboon mascot, like monkey roadkill.

"Very funny," I said.

"C'mon, get with the program," said Queenie. She grabbed my arm and hoisted me up the steps of the bus.

I ambled down the aisle. Teachers filled the front. I noticed a moony Nurse Supial gazing across the aisle at Coach Stroganoff, who was talking with the principal.

Natalie was jammed into the back with the other cheerleaders. The only free seat was by Jim Schortz, the cheery chuckwalla.

I slipped in beside him.

"Hey, dude," he said with a broad grin. "Ready to rock and roll?"

"How can you be so happy?" I asked. "Those missing players are still missing, and we're no closer to finding them than we were yesterday."

Jim *tsk-tsk*ed. "Don't worry. I have a feeling they'll turn up soon."

"And it doesn't bother you that we don't stand the chance of a snow cone in a sauna against Petsadena?"

The assistant coach shook his head like I was the slowest student in class. "The game's not over till it's over, dude."

Optimism makes me grumpy.

I sighed and turned to rest my cheek against the window. Jim's heavy hand landed on my shoulder.

"Cheer up, Chet," he said. "Hey, you know how hard you got tackled in practice this week?"

"Yeah?" I said.

"Well, those Petsadena players are gonna hit you twice as hard." He chortled and slapped me on the back. "Welcome to the big leagues, dude!"

Big league, schmig league. If I survived this game, I vowed never to play anything more athletic than checkers.

If I survived this game.

20

The Perils of Petsadena

Petsadena Elementary wasn't much to look at. It lacked the breathtaking views of Mount Everest, the glitter of the Taj Mahal, or even the sheer size of the pyramids.

It was an average school, for a palace.

It managed to make Emerson Hicky look like a bunch of tar-paper shacks in a swamp.

My teammates gawked as we shuffled down the hallways toward the gym. After we suited up, Jim Schortz gave us the signal. He pushed the door open and we streamed past him into the stadium.

The field was a long slab of green, as pure as a preschooler's prayer. Chalk lines gleamed against it, but not as much as the silver-uniformed Petsadena Baboons. Their outfits put the *twink* in *twinkle*.

The crowd's noise pressed against us like a little sister on a long car trip. The stands shook with hundreds of kids and parents from both schools, raising a ruckus.

My teammates waved as we trotted across the track to the benches.

Our stand-in quarterback, Brick the hedgehog, swaggered out to the fifty-yard line. By time-honored tradition, the two team leaders played rock-paper-scissors. In a close match, Brick's scissors beat the other guy's paper.

Petsadena would kick off.

Coach Stroganoff marched down our line, choosing the starting players. "Gecko—er, I mean, Stinky Bottomchucker, you've got bench duty," he growled.

Fine by me. While everyone else was wrapped up in their football thing, I could focus on my strength: the detective thing.

The teams took the field while I surveyed the scene. Behind me, the bleachers rocked with Emerson Hicky fans. Our band made a sound like a warthog choking on a xylophone. To this lopsided beat, a couple of cheerleaders began flinging around a dummy of Petsadena's baboon mascot, kicking it gleefully.

"Wow, check out *their* setup!" It was Natalie, leaning over my shoulder and pointing across the field.

On the other side, an army of Petsadena fans swelled the stands. Cheerleaders in shiny costumes danced a supersonic can-can, backed by the Petsadena Sympathy Orchestra.

"What, no fireworks?" I said.

Just then, red, silver, and black streaks shot into the sky, bursting into flowers of fire. A stunt plane spelled out PETSADENA RULES! with its smoke trail.

Something caught my attention in front of the enemy's bleachers. "Natalie, what's that?"

"That," she said, "is a pronoun, used to indicate something, like *that bench,* or *that cloud.*"

I grimaced. "No, down-for-brains, what's *that*?" I grabbed her beak and pointed it toward a line of figures. "Use your eagle eyes."

"Mockingbird eyes. Please." She squinted. "Huh. They've even got us beat in the mascot department."

"What do you mean?"

"I see one, two, three . . . six dummies of our gopher mascot, hanging from the stands."

What the Petsadena cheerleaders had planned for those dummies, I didn't want to know. Probably something involving cannons and farm machinery.

Pock!

The sound of a football being booted grabbed our attention.

"Go, Gophers!" shouted Natalie in my ear. "Sorry," she said, wincing. "Cheerleader training."

Petsadena had kicked off, and our team staggered around the field like blind mice on ice, trying to capture the ball. At last, P. Diddley fell on it. Four beefy beavers from Petsadena promptly fell on him.

Yikes.

The ball was at our own twenty-yard line. Both teams huddled—except for P. Diddley. He lay on the ground for the longest time, then wobbled to his feet, swayed like a hula girl in a hurricane, and ralphed up his lunch onto the grass.

"Ah, reminds me of Mom's home cooking," said Natalie from behind me.

Jim Schortz and Buford the skunk hustled onto the field and dragged P. Diddley off while the referees dealt with the stinky mess.

"Glad I'm not playing," I muttered.

A heavy paw fell on my shoulder.

"We can change that right now, bucko," grunted Coach Stroganoff. "You're up. Get out there and make your school proud!"

21

Tackling Dummies

My wobbly legs carried me onto the field. A couple of Petsadena players snickered as I passed them. An enormous badger growled.

"Nice doggie," I said.

He feinted at me with a razor-edged paw, and I dodged away. One day, my mouth would land me in trouble. (Worse trouble than being on the football team, I mean.)

Emerson Hicky's players crouched with their heads together. As I slipped into the huddle, Brick was calling the next play.

"Okay, Heavy Dogswater," he said, pointing to Queenie. "I want you—"

"I'm not Heavy Dogswater, I'm Raging Eggplant," she said.

"Right, Raging Eggs...water." Brick frowned.

"Eggplant," said Queenie.

"Whatever!" Brick's spikes stood on end. "You fake left and run a buttonhook. Now, you," he pointed at a surly frog. "Grumpy Potsticker..."

"Mean Moisturizer," the frog said. He jerked his head at a ground squirrel. "*He's* Grumpy Potsticker."

"Nuh-uh," said the squirrel. "I'm Flaming Spud-sucker, *he's*—"

"*I don't care!*" Brick hissed. "You. Frog. Run a zigzag on the left."

Queenie pouted. "But who gets the ball?" she asked.

Brick stabbed a finger at me. "Him."

"What?" said the frog.

"What?" said the squirrel.

"What?" said Queenie.

"You're kidding," I said.

Brick grinned. "Nope. They won't expect it— that's why it'll work. Team, ready..."

"Break!" everyone shouted, clapping their hands. They ran into position.

I crouched beside Brick, shaking my head. "You're bonkers," I whispered.

"No duh," he muttered. "Just run with it."

I wondered if it was too late to switch to the golf team.

On cue, the center hiked the ball. Brick faked, then handed off to me.

His spikes stabbed my palm. *Yowch!* I flinched. The ball fell from my hands and bounced crazily.

Huge Petsadena players tore through our line like sharks through a seafood buffet. Stagger-stepping after the ball, I drew a bead and—*zzthwip!*—snagged it with my tongue.

The chase was on!

Tongue wrapped around the ball, I sprinted for the sidelines. Forget about preserving yardage—I just wanted to preserve life and limb.

Ducking and weaving, I evaded a badger and a

wombat. I was only three steps from the line, when—*bam!* A marmot blindsided me.

Amazingly, I hung onto the ball. We sailed over the Petsadena bench, hit the track, and rolled—*bibbidy-fibbidy-bibbidy-whomp!*—until something hard stopped me.

All was spinning darkness.

I heard faint music, a heavenly choir.

Was I dead?

My jaw was wrapped around something big. *Hmm.* Unless they serve football-sized bugs in heaven, I was still alive. I carefully unfolded my body and unwrapped my tongue from the ball.

"Thanks," it seemed to say. "Kinda sticky."

"Don' men...shun it." I pushed my helmet off my eyes. Stars danced all around. The world throbbed to the beat of my heart.

Strange, furry shapes dangled above me. Was this a bat cave? The football didn't think so.

From the corner of an eye, I recognized the football field and some referees. The other direction, I saw lots of feet. My momentum had carried me up against the Petsadena stands.

That meant the furry shapes above must be the six mascots.

I sat up, bonking my head on a dummy. "Ouch!" it said in a muffled voice.

Pretty fancy, I thought, *even better than my sister's Little Wetsy doll.* The football agreed with me.

Then the referees arrived, along with Jim Schortz. They helped me stand and walked me across the field. They even took the football, who didn't seem to mind.

"Bye, foo'ball," I said, waving.

I felt just swell . . . like a terminal case of measles.

"Way to go, Gecko," said Brick as I limped past. "You gained two yards."

"An' I losth five teeth," I joked back, trying to make my tongue work.

Natalie and Shirley Chameleon were waiting by the bench, worried eyes big as soup bowls. As we drew near, Jim Schortz asked, "You okay, dude?"

"Thsure, I'm great," I said. "My tongueth's thstretched, my body acheths, and now I hear footballs and mathscoths talking to me."

The assistant coach chuckled. "Mascots talking?" he repeated. "Riiight."

"What do you mean?" asked Natalie. She reached out to help me sit.

I told them how the dummy had spoken when I bumped it.

"No fair," said Shirley. "They've got better mascots than us."

Jim said, "Whoa, that's weird," then mouthed

something to Natalie that looked like *Humor him*. "Listen," he said, "I gotta go help Buford suit up. He's taking your place."

Jim Schortz hustled off. After making sure I would recover, Shirley rejoined the cheerleaders, leaving me alone with Natalie.

My partner paced along the bench. "You know what's funny?" she said.

"That Coach ever believed I could play football?" I asked.

"Besides that," she said. "Why would Petsadena spend all that money on talking dolls? I mean, they're just going to throw the things around..."

My head started to clear. "And who could hear them over the orchestra and the cheerleaders, anyway?"

We fell silent.

Natalie looked at the field, where Buford had just joined the team. He took a handoff and ran for thirty yards before the other side tackled him. The Gophers cheered and pounded Buford on the back.

"Look at those poor dummies," I said. "They still think they can—"

"That's it!" she said. "They're not dummies!"

I shook my head. "Natalie, I know you take this cheerleader thing seriously. But you gotta face it: Most of my teammates aren't the brightest."

"Not your teammates," she said. "They *are* dummies. But I was talking about *those* dummies."

She pointed at the gopher mascots hanging from the Petsadena bleachers.

My eyes went wide. "You mean..."

"Partner, you found the missing players."

22

Gopher the Gusto

"Of course," I said. "Six mascots, six missing players. They probably knocked our guys out..."

Natalie nodded. "Then they stuffed them into gopher costumes and strung 'em up." She flapped her wings. "We've got to save them."

I looked past her. "We will. But first we drop the dime on the culprit."

Full of new energy, I limped over to Coach Stroganoff. "Coach, we found the missing guys," I said, pointing at the gopher dummies across the field.

The groundhog followed my gaze. His furry brow puckered in concern.

"Quite a hit you took there, Bottomchucker," he said. "Sure you're okay?"

"I'm fine, Coach," I fibbed. "And the name's Gecko—Chet Gecko. I have a confession to make. Don't be surprised..."

"Yes?"

"I'm not really a football player."

He nodded. "I'm not surprised."

"I'm a private eye," I said. "Going undercover was the only way to solve this case. And now I've found both the kidnap*ees,* and..." I pointed at Buford.

"The kidnapp*er,*" said Natalie and I together.

"Buford?" asked the coach.

"The same," I said.

We watched as the kidnapper in question caught a short pass and streaked down the field. Each time a would-be tackler approached, the skunk raised his tail and they backed off. In short order, he strutted across the goal line.

"Touchdown!" shouted Natalie. I caught her eye. "I mean, er, *bad* kidnapping football player!"

Beef Stroganoff clapped his massive paws. "Way to go, Skunk!" He turned back. "You just made a serious accusation. Got any proof?"

"Well, he's tight with this Petsadena football mom..." I looked around, noticing Jim Schortz talking to someone near the bleachers. "And *he* can help us prove it. Jim!" I called.

He and the Petsadena polecat looked our way.

"Hey!" said Natalie. "It's that football mom. What's she doing with Jim?"

The handsome chuckwalla flashed a quick grin and casually moved one paw behind his back. But not before I spotted a paper sack in it.

"And what's in that bag?" I asked.

"Good question," said Coach Stroganoff. He crooked a "Come here" finger at his assistant.

Jim shrugged his shoulders as the polecat edged away. The coach, Natalie, and I started slowly walking toward Jim. Just as slowly, he eased backward along the track.

We picked up the pace. So did Jim.

"What's happening?" asked Natalie.

"It's Private Eye Rule Number Twenty-seven, in action," I said.

"Which is?" asked Coach Stroganoff, breaking into a trot.

"If they run away, they're probably guilty," I said, trying to keep up. "Jim's in cahoots with Buford!"

This wasn't going to work. In my battered state, I couldn't run fast enough. Time for another play.

"Go get 'em, Coach!" I said. "Natalie, let's do an end-around pattern."

She frowned at me. "What's that?"

"Where you pick up my *end* and fly *around* to cut off Jim."

"What do you think I am, a passenger pigeon?" Natalie groused, but she flapped high enough so I could grab her legs, then took off.

Coach ran full tilt after Jim, who pounded down the track toward the exit. Natalie flew to intercept the speeding chuckwalla. Beneath us, football players looked up, confused.

"Ref, can they do that?" asked a Petsadena player.

Natalie panted with the effort of keeping us both airborne. "First thing...next week...you're dieting," she said.

"Aw, you're just sore because your boyfriend turned out to be a bad guy."

"He's not...my boyfriend!" she gasped.

We cleared the field. Jim had almost reached the gate.

"Go, Natalie!"

"Can't...hold you!"

In the space of a heartbeat, Natalie's wings gave out. We plummeted right into the chuckwalla's path.

"Yaah!" someone cried. (It might've been me.)

Ga-blonk!

Jim Schortz tripped over a tangle of private eyes and sprawled headlong. His paper bag fell beside me.

Coach Stroganoff caught up and stood over Jim with paws on his hips. Natalie groaned and rolled over.

I opened the sack and upended it. Paper money tumbled onto the ground in a green blizzard.

"What's that?" said Natalie.

I looked over at the fallen chuckwalla. *"That,"* I said, "is a pronoun, used to indicate something, like *that guy's in big trouble.*"

23

For Love and Cake

Coach Stroganoff refused to let me confront Buford the skunk until the game ended. Crime is serious. But, after all, it's not as serious as football.

He did send a referee to release the missing players from the gopher costumes. Six groggy guys tumbled out.

"Proof enough for you?" I asked the coach.

"We'll see," he said.

We stood guard on a bummed-out Jim Schortz and watched as Buford and his deadly tail led Emerson Hicky to victory. At last, my cheering teammates carried him on their shoulders (carefully) over to where we waited.

"Great game, Furious Barcalounger!" shouted

Coach Stroganoff, patting the skunk on his back.

"Furious Barcalounger?" I asked.

Coach beamed. "I figured out his nickname while we were waiting."

Buford waved to someone in the growing crowd behind me. "See, Mom?" he said. "I did it!"

Somehow, this accusing-the-culprit part wasn't starting quite the way I'd planned. I jumped in.

"Nice game, Buford," I said, "for a crook."

"What?" he asked.

"You conspired with Petsadena and Jim Schortz to kidnap those players."

My teammates muttered, confused. Coach watched with arms folded.

Buford bared his teeth. "Are ya nuts, or just jealous?" he said. "I didn't kidnap nobody."

"Don't lie," said Natalie. "We saw you after practice, talking to that lady polecat from Petsadena."

"But—" said Buford.

"She made stomachache pills in the pharmacy," I said, "and gave them to you. Then she paid off Jim Schortz to help, didn't she?"

The skunk looked from me to Natalie to the assistant coach. "Paid off . . . ?"

Jim looked away.

I hefted the money sack. "And here's the evidence, you crook."

Coach Stroganoff raised a thick eyebrow. "Well?" he asked. "What do you have to say?"

Buford's eyes searched the crowd. At last they locked on someone.

"Mom?" he said.

I followed his stare. There stood the Petsadena football mom—a black polecat looking guiltier than a kindergartner in a cookie jar.

"*That's* your mom?" asked Natalie.

"I'm adopted," said the skunk. "Mom, how could ya do it?"

She blushed. At least, I think she blushed. It's hard to tell on a polecat.

"Sweetheart, I just wanted you to play," said Buford's mother.

Buford sighed, exasperated. "Mo-om. I told ya, I can do it myself!"

Once the football mom confessed, the rest was easy. A mopey Jim Schortz admitted his part. With help from the polecat, he'd doctored several sticks of team gum with a chemical that made you sick and woozy.

"Of course!" I said. "Then you pretended you were taking the sick guys home, but you really brought them here."

"The Petsadena football moms kept them safe in

the toolshed and put knockout drops in their chocolate milk every day," said the polecat. She seemed almost proud. "They were glad to help."

I frowned at Jim. "So you sold out your team, kidnapped students, and disguised them as mascots—all so Buford could play?"

"It was the moms' idea to dress up the dudes like gophers," said the chuckwalla. He hung his head. "But the rest... yeah, I did it."

Natalie asked, "But why?"

Jim Schortz fingered his silk shirt. "Costs a lot to look this good."

"And your little scheme is going to cost you a lot more," said Coach Stroganoff. He grabbed Jim's arm in one paw and the polecat's in the other. "Let's go."

Before he could leave, Marge Supial parted the crowd. "Oh, Beefie," she said. "You're so forceful."

The big groundhog leaned close to her. "Not now, Smootchie-Poo," he muttered. "Beefie's busy."

Her face fell.

"But he won't be tonight," whispered Coach Stroganoff with a wink.

Nurse Supial brightened and kissed him on the cheek. *Yuck,* more mushy stuff.

As Beefie and his charges started off, up staggered my long-lost client, a slightly woozy Herman the Gila Monster. "Um, Coach?" he said.

Beef Stroganoff squared his mighty jaw. "Herman, I owe you an apology. Get back on the team, mister." He dragged the culprits away to face their punishment.

I walked up to Herman. "And you owe me my fee," I said.

Herman frowned sleepily. "Oh, yeah?"

"Yeah," said Natalie. "Fair's fair. You hired us, we solved the case."

The big lug thought about that. We waited. And waited. And waited. At last, he nodded. "Fair's fair, Gecko," he said. "Tomorrow, three cakes for you." The brute turned to go.

"Uh, Herman?" I said. "I think you mean *six* cakes—one for every player."

He turned back, wearing an expression that put the *ugh!* in *ugly.* "Three cakes, and I no break you in half for getting Herman kidnapped."

"Three cakes it is," I said, and shook his meaty paw. Ah, the negotiation game.

Herman trundled off to join his girlfriend, a dainty kangaroo rat. I knew that after tomorrow, we'd be back to bully and prey. But for now, Herman was another satisfied client.

"Three cakes," said Natalie, grinning.

"Three cakes," I agreed.

That was enough so that Natalie and I could have

our cake and eat it, too. Then have some more cake and eat it, too.

(I never really understood what that saying is supposed to mean, but as long as there's cake, who cares?)

Will Chet Gecko get his just desserts?
Find out in
The Malted Falcon

"Just what is this moldy falcon everyone's so excited about?" I asked. "Some birdy's funky old grandma?"

Freddie Nostrils sniffed. "It's the *Malted* Falcon," said the wiry prairie dog. "You mean nobody told you?"

I shook my head. "What's the Malted Falcon?"

"Er, think of the biggest dessert you can," he said.

"You don't know Chet Gecko," I said. "I can think of a pretty big dessert."

And I did. With pleasure.

Watching me, the prairie dog smiled. "Now triple it."

My eyes grew wide, picturing mountains of chunky weevil ice cream topped with snowcapped peaks of whipped cream. Candied grasshoppers did lazy backstrokes in lakes of fudge.

I think I started to drool.

"Er, Chet?" Freddie said. "Still with me?"

"Uh-huh."

"Excellent. Now, imagine having this dessert once a week . . . for a full year."

I blinked. "That's heaven."

Freddie leaned toward me. "No, it's not," he said. "That's the Malted Falcon."

"I don't understand."

The prairie dog paced. "I don't know if I can trust you," he muttered.

"Funny, that's what Principal Zero always says."

I waited for the nervous little rodent to make up his mind. At last, he faced me.

"You know that fancy candy shop at the mall . . ."

"Sweet Thang?" I said.

I knew the joint. They'd tossed me out a month earlier after I drank an entire Humungoloid Shake single-handed and danced the magic chicken mambo on the countertop.

Some shopkeepers have no appreciation for the arts.

"Yes, er, Sweet Thang," said Freddie, derailing my train of thought. "They've been giving out tickets to win the Malted Falcon whenever you buy a dessert. A, er, friend of mine got the winning ticket."

I swallowed my jealousy. "Lucky friend."

"Yes and no," he said.

"What do you mean?" I asked.

Freddie's buckteeth bared in a tight grin. "She, er, lost the ticket."

"Tough break," I said. "But what's all this got to do with me?"

The prairie dog fixed me with a bug-eyed stare. "I would like to hire you to find the missing ticket."

I was tempted, but . . . "Sorry, I'm already working a case."

Freddie stepped closer. "I'll double your fee," he said.

Double my fee would buy me another Humungoloid Shake (if I could get back into Sweet Thang). *Mmm.*

"Freddie," I said, "I'm your gecko."

"Excellent!"

"When should I start?"

The prairie dog reached into his book bag. His paw emerged holding a wicked-looking rubber-band gun. Loaded.

"How about right now?" said Freddie.

"What?"

He leveled the gun on me. "Hands up, please. We'll start by searching *you* for the ticket."

Look for more mysteries from the Tattered Casebook of Chet Gecko in hardcover and paperback

Case #1 *The Chameleon Wore Chartreuse*

Some cases start rough, some cases start easy. This one started with a dame. (That's what we private eyes call a girl.) She was cute and green and scaly. She looked like trouble and smelled like . . . grasshoppers.

Shirley Chameleon came to me when her little brother, Billy, turned up missing. (I suspect she also came to spread cooties, but that's another story.) She turned on the tears. She promised me some stinkbug pie. I said I'd find the brat.

But when his trail led to a certain stinky-breathed, bad-tempered, jumbo-sized Gila monster, I thought I'd bitten off more than I could chew. Worse, I had to chew fast: If I didn't find Billy in time, it would be bye-bye, stinkbug pie.

Case #2 *The Mystery of Mr. Nice*

How would you know if some criminal mastermind tried to impersonate your principal? My first clue: He was nice to me.

This fiend tried everything—flattery, friendship, food—but he still couldn't keep me off the case. Natalie and I followed a trail of clues as thin as the cheese on a cafeteria hamburger. And we found a ring of corruption that went from the janitor right up to Mr. Big.

In the nick of time, we rescued Principal Zero and busted up the PTA meeting, putting a stop to the evil genius. And what thanks did we get? Just the usual. A cold handshake and a warm soda.

But that's all in a day's work for a private eye.

Case #3 *Farewell, My Lunchbag*

If danger is my business, then dinner is my passion. I'll take any case if the pay is right. And what pay could be better than Mothloaf Surprise?

At least that's what I thought. But in this particular case I bit off more than I could chew.

Cafeteria lady Mrs. Bagoong hired me to track down whoever was stealing her food supplies. The long, slimy trail led too close to my own backyard for comfort.

And much, much too close to my old archenemy, Jimmy "King" Cobra. Without the help of Natalie Attired and our school janitor, Maureen DeBree, I would've been gecko sushi.

Case #4 *The Big Nap*

My grades were lower than a salamander's slippers, and my bank account was trying to crawl under a duck's belly. So why did I take a case that didn't pay anything?

Put it this way: Would *you* stand by and watch some

evil power turn *your* classmates into hypnotized zombies? (If that wasn't just what normally happened to them in math class, I mean.)

My investigations revealed a plot meaner than a roomful of rhinos with diaper rash.

Someone at Emerson Hicky was using a sinister video game to put more and more students into la-la-land. And it was up to me to stop it, pronto—before that someone caught up with me, and I found myself taking the Big Nap.

Case #5 *The Hamster of the Baskervilles*

Elementary school is a wild place. But this was ridiculous.

Someone—or some*thing*—was tearing up Emerson Hicky. Classrooms were trashed. Walls were gnawed. Mysterious tunnels riddled the playground like worm chunks in a pan of earthworm lasagna.

But nobody could spot the culprit, let alone catch him.

I don't believe in the supernatural. My idea of voodoo is my mom's cockroach-ripple ice cream.

Then, a teacher reported seeing a monster on full-moon night, and I got the call.

At the end of a twisted trail of clues, I had to answer the burning question: Was it a vicious, supernatural were-hamster on the loose, or just another science-fair project gone wrong?

Case #8 *Trouble Is My Beeswax*

Okay, I confess. When test time rolls around, I'm as tempted as the next lizard to let my eyeballs do the walking . . . to my neighbor's paper.

But Mrs. Gecko didn't raise no cheaters. (Some language manglers, perhaps.) So when a routine investigation uncovered a test-cheating ring at Emerson Hicky, I gave myself a new case: Put the cheaters out of business.

Easier said than done. Those double-dealers were slicker than a frog's fanny and twice as slimy.

Oh, and there was one other small problem: The finger of suspicion pointed to two dames. The ringleader was either the glamorous Lacey Vail, or my own classmate Shirley Chameleon.

Sheesh. The only thing I hate worse than an empty Pillbug Crunch wrapper is a case full of dizzy dames.

Case #9 *Give My Regrets to Broadway*

Some things you can't escape, however hard you try—like dentist appointments, visits with strange-smelling relatives, and being in the fourth-grade play. I had always left the acting to my smart-aleck pal, Natalie, but then one day it was my turn in the spotlight.

Stage fright? Me? You're talking about a gecko who has laughed at danger, chuckled at catastrophe, and sneezed at sinister plots.

I was terrified.

Not because of the acting, mind you. The script called for me to share a major lip-lock with Shirley Chameleon—Cootie Queen of the Universe!

And while I was trying to avoid that trap, a simple missing-persons case took a turn for the worse—right into the middle of my play. Would opening night spell curtains for my client? And more importantly, would someone invent a cure for cooties? But no matter—whatever happens, the sleuth must go on.